St. Francis Xaviers College

Pearls Of A Year

Short Stories

St. Francis Xaviers College

Pearls Of A Year
Short Stories

ISBN/EAN: 9783741185076

Manufactured in Europe, USA, Canada, Australia, Japa

Cover: Foto ©Andreas Hilbeck / pixelio.de

Manufactured and distributed by brebook publishing software
(www.brebook.com)

St. Francis Xaviers College

Pearls Of A Year

Pearls of a Year.

SHORT STORIES

FROM

" THE XAVIER,"

1888.

WRITTEN AND PUBI ·······

BY THE

STUDENTS OF ST. FRANCIS XAVIER'S COLLEGE,

NEW YORK CITY.

P. J. KENEDY:
No. 5 BARCLAY STREET, NEW YORK.
1888. ω

Contents.

THE LITTLE HANDFUL OF PEARLS HERE GATHERED

IS PRESENTED TO OUR READERS

BY THE

STUDENTS OF ST. FRANCIS XAVIER'S COLLEGE,

THEY WERE PUBLISHED

AT VARIOUS TIMES DURING THE YEAR 1888,

AND SO WELL WERE THEY RECEIVED BY MANY KIND FRIENDS

THAT THEY WERE SELECTED

TO SHED THEIR MODEST BEAUTY NOT ONLY AMONG

OLD AND TRUE FRIENDS

BUT THROUGH THEM AMONG MANY OTHER

AND NEWER FRIENDS.

NEW YORK:

St. Francis Xavier's College,
Feast of St. Aloysius,
JUNE 21, 1888.

THE PEARLS OF A YEAR.

'88

This night there is a ship that seaward sails,
  Waiting her mariners; O ye untried!
  Who never yet beyond the quiet tide
Adventured, dare ye face the ocean gales,
Where timbers rend and over shrieks and wails
  The wild sea whelms? Yet well equipped are ye
For storm and hurricane, nor need to blanch
  Though dark the sky or billowy the sea.
Go, then, and fear not. Forth in courage launch.
  Forth! in the strength of manhood and of youth,
Forth! in the hopes that every heart impel,
  Forth! in the light of heaven—the love of truth!
I hear e'en as I speak the parting bell;
  Your God,—your faith,—your country. Go, farewell.

Mr. Rattler's Story.

"WELL, BELLE," said Miss Ella Sprightly to her cousin, Miss McThusalum, "don't you think it is insufferably dull this evening? I shall positively go to my room unless you girls propose something to pass away the time."

"I say," exclaimed her sister, Tot, "this is just the evening for a story. Come, Mr. Rattler, won't you favor us with one?"

"My dear Tot, a story! I have not told one since I was a very little boy, and was switched for my last."

" Nonsense ! I am speaking English.   I don't wish a 'fib,' but a tale
—an adventure.   Something æsthetic, or harrowing, or transcendental,
or diplomatic, or——"

" Oh, such big words !   Spare me ! "

" Big words !   Am I a primer, that I cannot speak in more than dis-
syllables without giving notice ?   Be comfortable, pray, and do as you
are bid."

" Bid ! " yawned Rattler.   He was sitting on the upper step of the
flight which led into the house, his head leaning back upon the door-
sill of the piazza, and his legs dangling down.   It must be confessed
that Mr. Rattler's manners were uncommon and various.   His very
best were very good, indeed, but he would not run the risk of wearing
them out by constant use ; his second best were tolerable ; his worst I
would not like to see.   At present he was indulging in his second best ;
for if his attitude lacked respect his tone was pleasant, and he was with
those who excused his manner for the sake of his matter, and covered
over his defects with the shady mantle of " oddity."

" Bid ! ' he yawned again.   " What kind of a story did you suggest ?
Diplomatic ?   Shall I tell you how, at the President's public reception,
I said : ' I wish you a long life, lots of fun, and a second term, your
excellency ; ' he answering, ' Thank you, sir ; ' and how circumstances
over which I, unfortunately, had no control, compelled me to go home,
not knowing if he really meant that he was willing to succeed himself ? "

" No, I won't have that anecdote ; for you have condensed the whole
thing, point and all, in your one sentence."

" Then you wish to be kept in suspense.   Oh, let me off ! "

Tot shook her head, and called out : " Gipsy, Mr. Rattler is going
to tell us a story.   Come and listen."

" I don't believe in stories worth hearing which you patronize or submit to me," answered Gipsy, joining the party.   " She sent me a book

lately," turning to Mr. Rattler, " written as an old fogy might talk, with her compliments as the author. I feel greatly obliged for the compliment to my understanding:"

"Oh ! had you been deceived by it," retorted Tot, " it would not have brought your wit into question—it would only have shown your appreciation of mine. It was to test your guage of me, not mine of you."

" That was fair enough," said Rattler. " if Tot has cause to doubt your valuation of her mental charms. But apropos of writing, I have a story which ought to be written——"

" Write it, then ; for, after all, you write better than you speak."

"Indeed ! " Rattler was put on his mettle by the malicious sparkle in the lively girl's eye, as she threw out this suggestion."

" I will tell it to you," he said.

He shook himself into a sitting posture, and there was a silence of some moments.

The light from the inner room scarcely reached the group, but a young moon danced upon the broad ocean, which rolled and surged and beat lazily upon the beach not a hundred yards from the house. Piles of sand drifted here and there and lay white and still in the cool but breathless calm.

There was no sound from any neighboring cottage, and nothing interfered with Rattler's strong and marked voice as he thus deliberately began :

" There is a narrow strip of land on my plantation which connects the island on which I live with the ' main.' 1 determined, during the last spring, to make a causeway there, and so facilitate communication between the two. I had a gang of laborers set to work at this spot, and one afternoon took my way, as usual, to see how the work was coming on. But 1 was late in starting. My pony stood saddled at the door, and I loitered, to play with my little girl, to watch the gambols of a litter of terriers, to light a fresh cigar, etc.   Finally, when under way, the evening had nearly closed in, and I pushed on to reach the causeway before night.

" A thicket of trees borders the road on either side as you approach this end of the island; jessamine vines interlace their branches, forming by day a perfect bower of amber sweetness, but at night producing a gloomy darkness which no moonbeams could pierce.

" My horse dropped into a walk as we skirted this narrow path, and my stirrup brushed aside the blossoms in our slow progress.   I was idly meditating another European journey, and thinking over the expense of it, when a hand, as cold as ice, laid itself upon mine.   Starting, I turned toward the thicket—everything was indistinct, but the lifeless hand lay heavily on my right, and the horse had stopped.   I passed my hand along the wrist of this strange apparition, and discovered an arm belonging to it ; but so wasted, so emaciated, so worn, that my first idea of its being one of my men fallen dead near me, passed from my mind.   None of my people could, unknown to me, have reached so miserable a state.   With an impulse, to which I instantly yielded, I drew the entire body from the entangled shrubbery, and tossed it, light as it was, across the pony's neck.   Urging him then to full speed, I pressed through the grove ; the daylight was nearly spent, and to my horror, I could just distinguish, as we cleared the overhanging trees and came into the open country, that the burden I partly bore was a shapeless mass, of which the head, crowned with golden hair, displayed features most beautiful, most pallid, and most ghastly.   Just then, to increase my anxiety, my horse began to labor, as if the weight oppressed him, and it seemed to me that I could feel an increased pressure in the side which leaned against me.   I gazed at the creature with an indefinable sensation—it was not merely the contact of a dead body—a supernatural horror seized me.   I would, I believe, have thrown off the terrible thing, but it moved and murmured, " The warmth—the delicious warmth ! " and drew closer to me, feebly gasping, not like a human being, but——

"Great God ! I can't describe it ! "

"Go on," cried his listeners, with shuddering attention, and "Tot " bent her head toward him, and glanced nervously behind her.

"It opened its eyes and fixed them upon me with a steady look—so earnest, so despairing, so deep, so unnatural, that I trembled, and all my courage fled. I would have screamed like a woman, for my horse now began to snort and shiver, and a cold sweat bathed his limbs. This must be some devilish device. I struck my booted heel into his clammy flank, and tried to urge him on. Then, for the first time, I saw that I had lost my way ; we were not approaching the house—we had not the path to the men's quarters ; but, turn the bridle as I would, we were re-entering the thicket of jessamines.

"The black night had fallen, and close to me clung this horrible presence, growing heavier each instant, and filling me with such thoughts as a life-time will not efface. The gaze of those hopeless eyes—the pressure of that dead hand ! I could stand it no longer. I was about to fling myself from my horse in despair, when the creature raised one of those long, white emaciated arms which gleamed in the darkness, and laid it on my shoulder. It chilled my very marrow. I shook it off, and the voice said : ' What, ungentleness in you ! At the sound, my horse's feet refused to move ; he staggered, tumbled and stood still. I felt the unearthly breath of the dead mass upon my cheek, hissing in my ear. I struggled—what a moment of agony ! and—and—" Go on," said Tot. " Please do ! " cried Gipsy. "I cannot, said Mr. Rattler ; the secret of that night must be mine for ever. You have asked me for a story—of that one I can never tell another word."

"Oh," cried Tot, " I shall never ask you for a story again. You have frightened me heartily ; for even if it were nothing in itself, your man-

ner of relating it was so admirable, your dramatic effect was so perfect,
I sat thrilled and miserable.   What a raconteur!"

" Then I *can* speak as well as write? " said Mr. Rattler, with his third
yawn.

The Story of a Life.

TOWARD the close of our struggle for freedom, and deep within the
blue hills of New Hampshire, there dawned in 1782, the life of
one who was to be a power in the young republic, who was to guide the
destinies of the nation, to be wise in the councils of the wise, and
cherished in the hearts of men.   While the founders of the nation were
solving the great problem of its existence, seeking to mature and
strengthen the powers of the young state, which has now grown into
the giant of the west, he who was born with it grew strong and brave
and hardy among the open hills of his birth place.   He was mountain-
bred and his liberty was sweeter to him than the fresh breath of the
hills.

Webster loved the rude scenes of his childhood, the fields, crowning
with their hard-won grain, the labor of the year, the laden orchards, the
cooling woods, the grand mountains, raising their clouded tops in glory
to the heavens.   His young spirit raised up, like the mountains, golden
hopes toward the great and the boundless.   There was that in him
which told him he had something which was sought of men—a powerful
mind, and a priceless gift of eloquence to speak that mind.   And in
his heart there came a yearning for a station high among the children of
men, and an honored place in their memories.

Thus ambition entered into the young life, and it served never so
good a purpose, for it shaped that life to a noble end.

Years passed on, and strong and steady was the toiling both of mind and body. Daniel Webster passed from the hills of the country to the city and to college. Often did he lose courage in himself, when he saw how feeble he was to express the thoughts that rose in him ; but he applied himself more and more to the study of the success of others. His mind was enriched with the treasure of the past ; he grew in power, and the new strength gave him a new courage to rely on a well-trained mind.

He left college and went forth among the sons of men. Of all pursuits open to him, the service of the state, with which he was born, had most attracted him. It best opened the way for that leadership of men, which had been his boyish aspiration and was now his man's ambition. He was strong with the people, because of his kind heart and his noble eloquence ; and so, though still in his youth, he was enrolled among the leaders of the land. Here he soon had an opportunity to display his matchless power of speech. His talent was immediately recognized, and the name of Webster was noised over the land. Time and time again his eloquence was heard ; his long labor was crowned with success at last, and he was the acknowledged peer of American speakers. He entered the senate and the day of his greatest honor was come, the day when the brightest ·and most precious stone was set in his diadem of glory.

Taking advantage of his rival's press of work, Col. Hayne, a brilliant southern orator, made an insidious attack on the union and a bitter one on the north. It was totally unexpected. It fell like a thunderbolt among the startled legislators, and left them astounded and amazed. Who, on such short notice, would dare face that well prepared orator ? Webster was not wanting. Like an heroic knight of old he would plant himself full in the deadly breach, beat off all attacks, and win the glorious day against the enemies of freedom.

Webster was to answer ! The senate was crowded with fearing friends, but he was calm and confident. He knew he was right, and that consciousness gave him unspeakable strength. It were idle to describe the scene—to say with what a master's touch he played on the hearts of his hearers—to call again to mind the laughing faces, as they became fixed in thought, the laughing eyes changing to an earnest glow, and then melting away into tears before the pathos of his eloquence! When he finished with that great appeal for liberty and union, the senate rang with such a shout as never was heard before. All over the land the cry of praise was taken up ; the Pacific rolled out its majestic approval, while the Atlantic thundered its proud acclaim, and bore away over its stormy bosom tidings of the great speech. It will be never forgotten, that grandest effort in behalf of our freedom.

For years yet, until 1852, the eloquent voice was heard, ever thundering in behalf of the mighty nation to which it was consecrated. And when at last, the three score and ten of the just man were completed, the voice was silenced at the post of duty, and he passed to his greater reward.

Glory to Daniel Webster ! Glory to the brave, strong man, the ideal American, who raised himself by the mere force of genius, from among the lowest even to the highest ! His name is burned in love on the heart of every patriot. Imperishable is it written on the list of the unforgotten, on the list of the good and the great. Bright and fixed as the north star in the heavens, he stands before us for all time, the Prince of American orators.

Frederic Ozanam.

A MONG the brilliant men who have led the onward march of French genius during the 19th century, who have won renown for their loyalty to Religion and Truth, and who have moulded the intellectual destinies of our age, there is one name of deep interest to the thoughtful student. That name is Frederic Ozanam. In all our schools of philosophy, theology and poetry, among our ecclesiastics, our moralists, our politicians, and our critics, the influence of Ozanam has worked, though silently and unseen, yet with widespread and mighty effect.

His name makes the heart glow, for it opens to our mind unlimited and fruitful fields of reflection, commands serious, important, and thickly crowding thoughts, and forms a centre round which numberless subjects of discussion and investigation are collected. To fully and adequately describe his life and works is beyond human power, but the few testimonies and the fact that his genius and intellect have aroused the spirit of faith in France, are sufficient to convince us of the power our hero possessed.

Frederic was born at Milan in 1813, and died in 1853. His family was descended from the noble Jewish family of Hozannam. The stamp of genius, so marked in all his ancestors, shone none the less brilliantly in Frederic, for he bore everything away by the power and authority of his genius and the intensity of his convictions. The first recollections we have of him is of a noble, intelligent youth launched in a great university, subjected to the attractions of heretic principles; again we see him winning the highest honors of the class by his wisdom and genius; and finally a hero refuting and destroying the shrewd objections of the Voltairean and Rationalistic schools. From his earliest years one thought was constantly before his mind, namely, to kindle in France the devotion to religion and Christian courage, which in young hearts shine more brilliantly than all victories. The reason for his ardent spirit, we find in one of his letters addressed to a friend, describing the relief from his unceasing doubts: "I believed henceforward with an assured faith, and, touched by this mercy, vowed to consecrate my days to the service of that truth which had given me peace."

While at the university he organized a debating society, and as he was not the man for half measures, he devoted no little time to its advancement. The result can easily be drawn from the words of his biographer on this point: "It was impossible," he says, "to listen to him on the most difficult or uninteresting subject and not feel both moved and enchanted." His style of delivery was entirely Socratic, gaining the minds of his hearers by his reason and his earnest delivery. In the history of his life we learn of his entering the Sorbonne, whose walls had re-echoed the dangerous and senseless theories of Voltaire and others for nearly half a century, and there discussing their principles and forcing his opponents to admit the superiority and truth of his doctrine. Even in the midst of all his achievements he was not led astray by his ambition, for he well knew that everything must give way before the power and authority of those devoted to truth.

The year 1841 was a period of intense intellectual anarchy, and a strong hand was needed to stem the current, hence in his twenty-eighth year he was appointed assistant professor at the Sorbonne. It was in this office that his powers appeared brightest, for he clothed the rich stores of his knowledge with a rare diction, and not only instructed but refined the minds of his pupils. We have to regret that so few of his lectures have come down to us; but in what we have we can trace a true and clear philosophic mind. The best known of Ozanam's writings, and that which shows the real tenderness and grace of his ardent faith is "Dante et la Philosophie Catholique."

Although he devoted his life to literature, yet he was esteemed by all as a devoted and warm patriot, constantly ready to lend his voice to

the success of a true political measure. It might seem dangerous for
a man of Ozanam's ardent religious principles to teach an audience
where the opponents of the Catholic church largely predominated; but
the young hero feared no danger, and fortune, ever willing to crown
the brave, stood by the intrepid champion of the faith. The student
who has not read the life of Ozanam, has missed one of the choicest
biographies of manly character yet published. Forty years of open,
manly bearing, of unspotted life and high Christian virtues, have left
for him a rich and unfading memory. Lacordaire, in speaking of him,
says. "He had a charm which added to his other gifts, completed in
his person the artisan of a predestined enchantment. He was gentle
to all men, but just towards error." Thus, we see in him a model of all
Christian perfection, with a heart full of the true spirit, as ready to
offer his life for the defence of one jot or tittle of the faith. In the
words of Cardinal Manning, "May God raise up on every side laymen
like Frederic Ozanam."

The Story of Judith.

Soft chants the turtle in Bethulia's vale,
And gently nods the olive to the moon ;
The mirth of timbrels is no longer heard,
And silent is the harp's rich melody ;
The sacrifice is done, the night watch set,
Grim darkness has come on and wearied all ;
And dreams are stealing o'er each soldier's tent.

Down thro' the valley ran a limpid stream,
With myrtle, citron-palm and cypress lined ;
And there beneath the stars fair Judith prayed,
And fair beyond the word she was, for God

Had stamped the beauty on her brow, that led
A captive, Holofernes' wayward heart,
And freedom gave her woeful native land.

She placed aside her widow garb, and clad
Herself in white; her sandals were of silk,
Her raven hair she plaited in a crown,
Her bracelets and her ring were crusted gold;
Her liquid eyes shone dark and beautiful,
And these she screened beneath her bridal veil,
While thus, with hands outstretched she prayed to God.

" O Lord, lift up Thy arm and crush Thy foes,
They strive by might to rob Thy dwelling place,
They violate Thy sanctuary and defile
Thy hallowed altars; yet Thy power is not
In mighty hosts, nor in the spear, nor steed.
Then strengthen me! that all the world shall say
That Thou art King and none is like to Thee."

With quickened step and holy thoughts she sped,
And at the tent of Holofernes' stood.
The taper flickered dimly, and the urn
Of incense spread the sweet and fragrant smoke.
She paused—then drew the silken canopy
That slumbered o'er the downy regal couch
And looked upon fierce Holofernes' face.

Like all the guards, sweet sleep had weighed his eyes;
His massive pike hung gleaming on the peg.
She stole the half-drawn sabre from his side:
Her lips were moved in prayer—" God strengthen me."
Then suddenly a blush passed o'er her face,
Quick flashed the sword—his lips and wild eyes closed.
The deed was done—Jerusalem was free.

We praise Thee, God! For o'er their camp Thine eye
  Had looked—It wearied them—dark night came on,
The deep had held their feet—the waters high
  Had swallowed them, their shields and spears; upon
The mountains, some an exile's song now sing
Unto their country and their warrior king.
  Maidens of Judah, and ye youths arise—
  Strike harp and sing her victory to the skies.

  " Thou art the glory of Jerusalem,
    Thou art the greatest joy of Israel,
    Thou art the honor of thy chosen land,
    Thou art the fairest flower of woman-kind."

That Terrible Night.

"DID you ever hear," said a friend once to me, "a real, true ghost
story, one you might depend upon?" "There are not many
such to be heard," I replied, "and I am afraid it has never been my
good fortune to meet with those who were really able to give me a
genuine, well-authenticated story." "Well, you shall never have cause
to say so again, and as it was an adventure that happened to myself,
you can scarcely think it other than well-authenticated. I know you to
be no coward, or I might hesitate before I told it to you. You need
not stir the fire; there is plenty of light by which you can hear it. And
now to begin: I had been riding hard one day in the autumn for
nearly five or six hours through some of the most tempestuous weather
which I ever had the ill-luck to meet. It was just about the time of the
equinox, and perfect hurricanes swept over the hills, as if every wind

in heaven had broken loose and had gone mad, and on every hill the
rain and driving sleet poured down in one unbroken shower.

"When I reached the head of Townshend Valley—you know the
place, a narrow ravine with rocks on one side, and those rich, full
woods (not that they were very full then, for the winds had shaken
them till there was scarcely a leaf on their bare, rustling branches) on
the other hand, with a clear little stream, winding through the hollow
dell—when I came to the entrance of this valley, weather-beaten vet-
eran as I was, I scarcely knew how to hold on my way. The wind,
held in, as it were, between the two high banks, rushed like a river just
broken loose into a new course, carrying with it a perfect sheet of
rain, against which my poor horse and I struggled with considerable
difficulty. Still I went on, for the village lay at the other end, and I
had a patient to see there who had sent a very urgent message, en-
treating me to come to him as soon as possible. We are slaves to a
message, we poor medical men, and I urged on my poor jaded brute,
with a keen relish for the warm fire and good dinner that awaited me
as soon as I could see my unfortunate patient, and get back to a home
doubly valued on such a day as that in which I was then out.

It was, indeed, dreary riding in such weather, and the scene
through which I was passing was certainly not the most conducive
toward raising a man's spirits ; but I positively half wished myself out in
it all again rather than sit the hour I was obliged to spend by the sick-bed
of the wretched man I had been summoned to visit. He had met with
an accident the day before, and as he had been drinking up to that
time, and the people had delayed sending for me, I found him in a
frightful state of fever, and it really was an awful thing to either look
at or to hear him. He was delirious and perfectly furious, and his
face, swelled with passion and crimson with the fever that was burning
him up, was a sight to frighten children, and not one calculated to add
to the tranquility even of full-grown men. I dare say you think me

very weak and that I ought to have been inured to such things, minding his ravings no more than the dash of the rain against the window ; but, during the whole of my practice, I had never seen man or woman, in health or in fever, in so frightful a state of furious frenzy, with the impress of every bad passion stamped so broadly and fearfully upon the face. And in the miserable hovel that then held me, with his old, witch-like mother standing by, the babel of the wind and rain outside added to the ravings of the wretched creature within, I began to feel neither in a happy nor enviable frame of mind. There is nothing so frightful as when the reasonable spirit seems to abandon man's body and leave it to a fiend instead.

"After an hour or more waiting patiently by his bedside, not liking to leave the helpless old woman alone with so dangerous a companion I thought that the remedies by which I hoped in some measure to subdue the fever, were beginning to take effect, and that I might take my leave of him. I promised to send all that was necessary, though fearing much that he had gone beyond all my power to restore him, and I asked to be called back immediately should he get worse instead of better, which I felt almost certain would be the case. Having performed this kindly service, I hastened homeward, glad enough to be leaving wretched huts and raving men, driving rain and windy hills, for a comfortable house, dry clothes, a warm fire and a good dinner. I think I never saw such a fire in my life as the one that blazed up my chimney ; it looked so wonderfully warm and bright, and there seemed an indescribable air of comfort about the room which I had never noticed before. One would have thought I should have enjoyed it all intensely after my wet ride, but throughout the whole evening the scenes of the day kept recurring to my mind with most uncomfortable distinctness. It was in vain that I endeavored to forget it all in a book, one of my old favorites, too, so at last I fairly gave up the attempt, as the hideous face kept continually rising before my eyes and an es-

pecially good passage, and I went off to bed heartily tired and expect-
ing sleep very readily to visit me. Nor was I disappointed. I was
soon asleep, though my last thought was on the little valley I had left.
How long this heavy and dreamless sleep continued I cannot tell, but
gradually I felt consciousness returning in the shape of the very
thoughts with which I fell asleep and at last I opened my eyes, thoroughly roused, by a heavy blow at my window. I cannot describe my
horror, when, by the light of a moon struggling among the heavy surge-
like clouds, I saw the very face, the face of that man looking in at me
through the casement, the eyes distended and the face pressed close to
the glass.

I started up in bed to convince myself that I really was awake, and
not suffering from some frightful dream. There it stayed, perfectly
motionless, its wide, ghastly eyes fixed unwaveringly on mine, which,
by a kind of fascination, became equally fixed and rigid, gazing upon
the dreadful face which alone, without a body, was visible at the win
dow. I can scarcely tell how long I sat looking at it, but I remember
something of a rushing sound, a feeling of relief, a falling exhausted
back upon my pillow, and then I awoke in the morning, ill and unre-
freshed.

I was ill at ease, and the first question I asked upon coming down
stairs, was whether any messenger had come to summon me to Townshend. A messenger had come, they told me, but it was to say I need
trouble myself no further, as the man was already beyond all aid, having died about the middle of the night. I never felt so strangely in my
life as when they told me this, and my brain almost reeled as the
events of the previous day and night passed through my mind in rapid
succession. That I had seen something supernatural in the darkness
of the night I had never doubted, but when the sun shone brightly into
my room in the morning, through the same window where I had seen
so frightful and strange a sight by the spectral light of the moon, I be-

gan to believe it had been a dream, and endeavored to ridicule myself out of all uncomfortable feelings. Haunted by what I considered a painful dream, I left my room, and the first thing I heard was a confirmation of what I had been for the last hour endeavoring to reason and ridicule myself out of believing. It was some hours before I could recover my ordinary tranquility, and then it came back, not slowly as you might have expected, as the impression gradually wore off, and time wrought his usual changes in mind as in body, but suddenly—by the discovery that our large white owl had escaped during the night, and had honored my window with a visit before he became quite accustomed to his liberty."

St. Francis Xavier.

HIS LIFE.

A WRITER of the present century, speaking of St. Francis Xavier, says that of his life one might write a poem that would be the epic of charity. To tell even the principal events of his wonderful life would require many pages, and consequently I have selected one of his many virtues, his unflagging zeal. Even when a young professor of philosophy at the University of Paris, he had excited the surprise of all by his energy and devotion to his work. His class-room was thronged with admirers who listened to his explanations of the lessons, and were surprised at his energy ; but there was one, the great Ignatius of Loyola, who could not help saying : " Xavier, this is for time—what are you doing for eternity ? " With these words came the call to be a priest, and the apostolic vocation of the young professor continued to grow from that very moment. He was never tired of laboring for souls, and when he received the order for his departure to the East, he would have gone without the necessary garments had not Loyola put his own cloak upon his shoulders.

To follow our great apostle through all the various provinces of the East which he traversed chiefly on foot, and to speak of all the miraculous powers which God gave him, would surpass my limits. But in every act of his life we can trace that undying zeal for the salvation of souls. No cry of human misery was in vain when addressed to him— he cared for the sick, worked for the living and buried the dead. There are few persons who love work for the sake of always doing something for their soul's welfare, but among these Francis Xavier is so prominent, that a 'Protestant has said of him : " From the days of Paul of Tarsus to our own, the annals of mankind exhibit no other example of a soul borne onward so triumphantly through distress and dangers in all their most appalling aspects." He took no pleasure in idleness, in the leisurely folding of the hands to rest, or letting the mind indulge in useless dreaming. His heart and soul was in his work, and from this desire came his pleasure to convert souls. Nor must we imagine that these labors made him sad ; on the contrary, the song of gladness was ever on his lips ; he underwent cold, heat, hunger and suffering ; his naked feet were often torn by the thorns and briers, and all for his great work, to win souls to God. This is the advice he gave to his associates : " There is always work to be done, and earnest toilers are always wanted. Day dreams and idle plans will not help our cause."

St. Francis Xavier has ceased to live, but his labors live after him, and they tell us that, as he was in life, so was he in death, He had sown the seeds of Christianity in India, Ceylon and Japan ; would he stop here ? No ; there were millions of pagans in China, and his heart is turned towards them. The voyage was to be a sorrowful one ; as *ever*, Xavier labors hard, but is at last overcome ; after great pain he is put ashore in a dying condition. He pressed his crucifix to his breast and died singing the last strophe of St. Ambrose's canticle : " In te, Domine, speravi, non confundar in æternum."

It is safe to say that no man's work was ever more successful than that of St. Francis Xavier, and if we are devoted and earnest like *him* in our duties, we, too, may hope to reach the end for which we are now laboring.   For, as the poet says :

> " He liveth long who liveth well,
>   All else is life but flung away.
> He liveth longest who can tell
>   Of true things truly done each day.
> They fill each hour with what will last.
>   Buy up the moments as they go,
> The life above, when this is past,
>   Is the ripe fruit of life below."

HIS CHARACTER.

IN NO living being is the tendency to hero-worship so strongly developed as in the growing boy. The young love virtue. It comes naturally to them.   They never think of doing a mean or wicked act; and to them every man, tall, strong and noble-looking, seems the very perfection of all that is grand and good.   How often do we hear a blue-eyed innocent exclaim : " O ! I wish I was a great big man like papa ! "   But, think you, would they utter this wish if they knew what weak creatures most men are ? They soon learn.   Their beautiful fancies are quickly shattered, as the flying years increase a little their knowledge of the world ; and then they see that all men do not spend their lives in helping the weak, slaying dragons, and bringing their fellows nearer the good, the true and the beautiful.

Now begins their search for the ideal man.   They must have some

one to venerate, some one to imitate. They place their affections on an older brother, or to the boy in the highest class ; but a frown ot unrighteous anger mars the brow of their idol, and they quiver in uncertainty. They feel as if they had lost some support ; the world appears cold and dark.

In many cases it happens, that just as these youthful votaries grow old enough to understand the foibles of their companions, the field of literature opens up to them. Then the valiant Knights of the Table Round receive the homage that must escape from their overfull hearts. But after a season, even these noble characters pall, for the fantastic creatures of an author's imagination cannot long satisfy anyone. They crave for real men of flesh and blood ; men who, like themselves, have lived in the world and been of the world ; men who, like themselves, have felt the numberless temptations of the world ; but men of whom it can with truth be said, that they

> " Bore through action's stormy field
> Honor's white plume and Virtue's spotless shield."

They read through histories, and among the small number of true heroes' they see, standing prominently out above the rest, the form of St. Francis Xavier.

Xavier, as a boy, rushed headlong into many of the scrapes a healthy, thoughtless lad meets with ; but he never for a moment tolerated an unkind or mean act, and, when he had grown into a cool, deliberate man, he chose the most self-sacrificing profession in existence, and adopted the most rigorous branch of that profession.

When the great truth dawned on him that God wanted him to be a soldier in His army, he took up arms and engaged in active warfare against the demons of error. He did not stay among his own countrymen, the people whom he knew and loved, nor did he remain with the other nations of Europe, whose customs he knew, and with whose civilization he was familiar. He journeyed among strangers, of whom he

had heard nothing but the unreliable reports of travellers, among whom
no missionary had ever preceded him, and whose civilization was to
him a thing strange and unpleasant.

A stranger in a strange land, he preached the Gospel of Truth to a
hostile people ; and, in the course of his life, baptised a million con-
verts—a work which in itself could only be accomplished by a man of
the greatest energy and perseverance, so exhausting is the merely
physical portion of it.   Yet Xavier performed this work in spite of all
the hindrances an ingenious nation could invent against a stranger
who was assailing all that they held most holy.   He broke down all the
false religion that had obtained so firm a foundation in the hearts of the
strong-minded heathens of India and Japan, and built up in its stead
the beautiful structure of our Catholic faith.

Cannot we learn a lesson from this great Apostle of the Indies.   If
we are looking for an exalted model to fashion our lives after, why need
we search further ?   This man left his friends, his home, his country, in
obedience to the call of God ; cannot we, then surrounded by our own
dear family, among people who, we well know, are willing to help us,
cannot we perform the slight labors we are called upon to do ?   Surely
it is not a hard task, to live in a city containing every comfort the brain
of man can devise, and make a little progress every day, without sin-
ning.   Yet ever and again we hear of men who become discouraged in
their struggles because a few obstacles confront them, and who cry out,
" life is not worth living."

St. Francis did not try to convert all the East at once ; neither must
we try to gain wealth or renown immediately.   The great Jesuit father
preached the good tidings to a modest number at first ; and labored on,
never thinking of giving up because success did not instantly crown his
efforts.   Then, we, too, if we would imitate him, must be satisfied to
journey a little at a time in the right direction.   Let each moment see
us lay aside a little for the future.   It need not be money ; if we can

say at the end of the week that we have learned something useful in broadening our mind and in solving for us the problems of life, then we have successfully imitated an illustrious model. His great virtue was zeal ; let us persevere in laying up treasures for this life and for the greater life to follow.

Do not think that St. Francis was another kind of being from us. He was not. We can all be great if we try. We may neither convert nations nor amass fortunes ; but we can all do good in our own way, and thus earn Heaven, and what greatness can equal that ?

His Death.

'Twas evening, and the sun in glory sank,
And on the crested wavelets as they played
He shed a radiance changing them to gold,
Until they touched a lonely barren isle
Whereon the beating surges foam and break.
There, 'neath a little shelter of sparse leaves,
A dying saint was laid ; his noble brow
Flushed with a deadly heat ; his breath in pain.
The burning eyes were strained to catch the line
Where sea and sky commingle into one,
Where beat the waves upon that eastern land
That he had prayed to die in, and to save
The myriad souls of men, so dead, so blind,
Who knew not of their Father and their God.
His heavy lids were closing ; icy chills
Crept o'er his limbs ; the agony was nigh ;
The sky grew dark, and on the winged winds
A hellish voice cried mocking in his ear :
" Vain is thy dying wish ! Vain was thy life !
Those realms are mine ; their worship is for me !

For me, Satan, for me their god, their king!
Ha! Did it profit thee to leave the world
To bear that cross and, bearing it, to die?
I tell thee, after all these years of toil,
Thy labor and thy prayers have been in vain."
Great Xavier's heart beat fainter; but his soul
Was still undaunted, and his faith was firm;
And from the parched and swollen lips there came:
"My God! My God! I will not now despair;
Jesu! Maria! help me in this hour!—
If from the labor of this life now o'er
Will come no fruits, O Lord, Thy will be done;
And let one mightier in Thy cause than I,
One holier in Thy law and in Thy ways,
Come to complete what I have left undone."
He said; then grew his face an ashy pale;
And from the portals of the heavens above
Death's angel issued with a waving palm;
When lo! from far beyond the angel's form
A blessed vision to his eyes appears!
There in the heavens toward the western line
Where sea and sky commingle into one,
The distant shores of China seemed to rise!
The cross uplifted on its highest hills
Was glittering in the sunlight! Xavier looked;
Saw the bright promise, and adored his God.
The lovely isle became a source of light;
Illumined paths shone forth as from the sun;
And where they fell sprang many a noble pile
To worship and to learning beetling high;
And o'er them all there blazed in golden words
The name of Xavier—loved by all the world.
Yet one there seemed more brilliant than the rest,
Far, far away in the land then scarcely known,

Implanted deep within the busy town
Where was to throb a glorious nation's heart,
There rose a temple fair and there a fane,
Where wisdom sat enthroned.   A warmer ray
Of love poured from the eastern isle
Upon that temple of the western world !
But this he saw not, yet indeed beheld
That his life's labor would not come to naught,
And heard a mighty voice on high proclaim,
As fled the vision from the sky above:
" Welcome my son from off the dreary earth,
Welcome my child who lived and died for me,
Welcome to bliss eternal in my realms,
Welcome, my child, thy work is done, well done "

*   *   *   *   *

Far to the east and bordering on the line,
The line where seem to meet the sea and sky,
There lies an isle, alone, among the waves,
Where all around the surges foam and break.
'Twas morning, and the sun in glory rose ;
The night, its stars and gloom erstwhile had sped ;
The sea was calm, the surges ceased to beat ;
The wind was hushed ; great Xavier's soul had fled.

His Grave.

Where dash the waves with hollow roar
On San Cian's lonely desert shore.
A simple cross uplifts its form,
And braves the anger of the storm ;

And marks the spot where Xavier lay
Upon his last and happiest day.
At midnight in the sable light,
And when the full moon glows in white,
Around this islet, broad and bleak,
The starving jackals plaintive shriek ;
The fierce hyena's laughter shrill
Comes sounding o'er the distant hill.
The solemn ocean seems to pant ;
The waves a funeral requiem chant.
When morning dawns, and scorching sun
Tells of new reigns of heat begun,
He shines upon that battered sign
Of man's redemption, cross divine ;
And touches with a distant ray
The snow-topped mountains, blue and gray.
Then frames in gold the lofty palm,
And dances on the water calm.
The savage bands that tarry there
Upon the sacred emblem stare,
With superstitious looks pass by,
Pursue their journey with a sigh.
The wily merchant, as he guides
His vessel through Pacific tides,
The emblem sees, on th' island faint,
And solemnly invokes the saint ;
Then trims his sails and speeds away,
And follows up the parting day.
But calm or storm, or cold or warm,
The waves the solem requiem form :
Or tempest's roar, or zephyr's hymn,
Or sunshine glow, or midnight dim,
The glassy waves in liquid tones
Dash on that shore with mingled moans,

And chant in unison a psalm.
Distinct and measured, low and calm,
And seem to say in harmony :
"Eternity! Eternity!
This saint has found his rest in thee."

Longfellow's Dream of Acadia.

IT WAS a sad time in Acadia. For a year past the English govern-
ment had been harassing the poor colonists, seeking everywhere a
cause for quarrel. They had sworn allegiance to England, these poor
peasants, and had in every way endeavored to keep their oath sacred ;
but all was in vain. Envious eyes had been cast on their smiling fields,
won from the "forest primeval" by so many years of toil ; and the min-
istry of George III. thought that it would be a fertile spot for a
flourishing colony.

So their doom was sealed, and a convenient opportunity was sought
to carry out the already pronounced sentence. Unhappily the wished
for chance was only too quickly afforded. Some few Acadians were
detected in negotiations with their French neighbors, and in what community are there not a few who dissent from general principles ? Had
justice alighted on these few guilty ones history would not have com-
plained ; the inhuman cruelty with which the whole people was treated
is the ground of protest.

Their whole country was ruthlessly desolated—uprooted in a single
day ; their homesteads, endeared to them by many a tie, were burned
before their eyes ; their goods appropriated by the Puritans without a
scruple ; their most sacred ties of kinship cruelly disregarded. Mothers
had been torn from their daughters, fathers from sons, brothers and
sisters carried to different vessels, lovers separated never to meet again

—all, disembarked at various parts on the coast, had been turned adrift in a stranger land, with prospects blacker than the black smoke that rose from their burning dwellings. Bitter was the lot of these unfortunates! Wandering ever through an unknown land searching for the lost loved ones from whom they were separated in that cruel parting from country and all. Some there were that died in that foreign land, died among strangers; but others, in the evening of life, found their way back to their native country, only in time to rest in death with their happier fathers.

On this theme Longfellow has written his immortal Evangeline. It is essentially a Catholic story, recognized as such by all critics and by the poet himself. Indeed, he seems to have tried to atone for the Catholic tendencies of this work by writing "The Courtship of Miles Standish." Yet, however beautiful may be the character of Priscilla, the heroine of this Puritan poem, she can by no means be compared for sweetness of disposition and strength and firmness of purpose to her Catholic sister, the fair Evangeline.

The poet begins in his happiest manner, by showing the security of the Acadians, till that fatal edict of George III. was issued against them.

> "Aloft on the mountains
> Sea fogs pitched their tents, and mists from the mighty Atlantic
> Looked on the happy valley, but ne'er from their station descended.
> There, in the midst of its farms, reposed the Acadian village.
> ....In the tranquil evenings of summer, when brightly the sunset
> Lighted the village street, and gilded the vanes on the chimneys,
> Matrons and maidens sat in snow-white caps and in kirtles
> Scarlet, blue and green, with distaffs spinning the golden
> Flax for the gossiping looms. ..
> Solemnly down the street came the parish priest, and the children
> Paused in their play to kiss the hand he extended to bless them.
> ...Anon from the belfry

> Softly the Angelus sounded, and over the roofs of the village
> Columns of pale blue smoke, like clouds of incense ascending,
> Rose from a hundred hearths, the homes of peace and contentment."

The poet introduces us to his heroine on the night of her betrothal to "Gabriel Lajeunesse, the son of Basil the blacksmith."

It was the fall of the year, that time of peace and plenty; the harvests had been all gathered in, and everything prepared for "a winter long and inclement." It was twilight. The evening star had risen and the herds were returning from the pasture. Within the great oak built farmhouse sat Evangeline's father.

> " Hearty and hale was he, an oak that is covered with snowflakes,
> White as snow were his locks, and his cheeks as blown as the oak leaves."

Near by sat the ever-busy Evangeline spinning flax for the loom, and happy beyond description, for this was a great night.

> " Fair was she to behold, that maiden of seventeen summers.
> ....But a celestial brightness—a more ethereal beauty—
> Shone on her face and encircled her form, when after confession,
> Homeward serenely she walked, with God's benediction upon her."

The sound of heavy feet is heard upon the porch, and the voice of Basil the blacksmith. In a moment more he enters and Gabriel with him. For three days an English fleet has lain in the harbor, their hostile guns trained on the village. The peasants are ordered to meet in the church, there to submit to the pleasure of his most gracious majesty, George III. So, both the old friends are anxious and troubled; but their utmost conjectures of ill fall far short of what was so soon realized. Another step on the stairs, not heavy and firm now, but light and uncertain, another voice too—the kind, cheery voice of the old notary. Soon the marriage contract is drawn up, "and the great seal of the law is set, like the sun, on the margin."

> " Meanwhile apart in the twilight gloom of a window's embrasure
> Sat the lovers and whispered together, beholding the moon rise

Over the pallid sea and the silvery mist of the meadows.
Silently one by one, in the infinite meadows of heaven,
Blossom the lovely stars, the forget-me-nots of the angels."

And they were happy; for they dreamt and spoke—O, how hopefully!
—of the bright future which they, alas, were not to see, of a long, happy
life, simple and innocent, such as their parents had passed. What a
rude awakening was in store for them! How soon would that strong,
brave youth be snatched from the sight of her he loved, never again to
behold her till, long years after, bowed with age and sickness, weary
with waiting and hope, his dying eyes should light once more on her
angel face and he should clasp her to his bosom—only in death! How
soon would that artless, untried village girl be called upon to face trials
the most cruel—the loss of country, parents, friends, betrothed; and
how brightly would her strong character shine forth in the bitter hour
of affliction!

It was done, that cruel deed, forever a foul blot on the fair fame of
New England. The well equipped war ships, the result of two years'
preparation, had taken these peaceable, unresisting peasants, and
treated them worse than the most cruel savage would treat his most
deadly foe.

Evangeline was bewildered and confused. Her father had died that
fatal night they left their home; he was lying on the desolate sea shore
and the ocean was chanting his requiem. And Gabriel?—what had
become of him? Was he, too, dead? No, surely not dead; and she
would find him yet. Day and night she thought of these two dear ones,
hoping, praying ever for strength and courage to bear her bitter lot.
At the happiest moment of her young life, when it seemed that her
brightest hope was realized, like a thunderbolt from a clear sky has
fallen this great affliction and left her stunned, confused, well-nigh crazed.
Wherever aught was heard of Gabriel, thither she flew, but an evil fate
pursued her and Gabriel had always gone before. Notice the white,

eager face with which she asks about her lover, and mark how her eyes flash hope when she thinks that she still may find him.

With this steadfast constancy she ever follows the wandering Gabriel, pursuing eagerly the slightest trace of him, hoping against hope to the end. How truly that dark night on the "father of rivers," when the lost one drifts past unnoticed, does her lover's instinct warn her of his presence:

> "O! Father Felician,
> Something says in my heart that near me Gabriel wanders."

And the good priest cheered her:

> "Daughter thy words are not idle ...
> Gabriel truly is near thee; for, not far away to the southward,
> On the banks of the Têche are the towns of St. Maur and St. Martins.
> There the long-wandering bride shall be given again to her bridegroom,"

How her heart is lightened with this hope! She has never allowed herself to hope with such certainty before. Bitter indeed will be the disappointment! The day flies swiftly past till that wondrous sunset, when,

> "Hanging between two skies a cloud with edges of silver
> Floated the boat, with its dripping oars, on the motionless water."

And from the woods

> "The mocking bird, wildest of singers,
> Shook from his little throat such floods of delicious music,
> That the whole air and the woods and the waves seemed silent to listen."

They have disembarked at St. Martins—a loud, glad cry rends the air, for the exiles have found their brethren. Basil the blacksmith is there, too, but Gabriel—has gone. O, the anguish of that news to Evangeline! To have watched and waited for years for that meeting with her lover, and then, her hope all but realized, to have the chance so rudely snatched away, as it seemed, forever. Forever! No, she was not conquered yet, to-morrow she would seek him again—God willing, she would find him yet.

Up the great river, through the greater forest, past raging torrents, through the almost impassable mountains, on, ever toiling on, following the faint trace of her lover. Miles and miles over the boundless prairies her tireless footsteps urge her—her life ever in danger from the wild beast and wilder savage—till at last she reaches a little mission in the heart of the red man's country, whence, only six days before, Gabriel had departed. In the summer he returns here, she is told, and she will wait for him.

But the summer came, and the winter, and the spring and the summer again, but no Gabriel. Far in the north, they say, he lives the life of a solitary hunter, a man cast down by some great sorrow. She will go to him, she thought, and after weeks of toil and hardship, penetrated the wilds of Michigan. "He is near, he is near," and a glad cry rose from that sorely tried heart. But when she approached, the cabin had fallen in ruins, and the hearthstone was cold and cheerless.

The years fly past. Evangeline's fair form is bowed with age, her hair tinged with gray, the features pinched and wan from sickness and sorrow; only her eyes remain unchanged, and from their lustrous depths there gleams a strange, wild yearning and flashes a quenchless hope.

> " Patience and abnegation of self, and devotion to others,
> This was the lesson, a life of trial and sorrow had taught her."

Thus she lived as a Sister of Mercy, visiting day after day the wretched hovels of the poor; comforting, consoling them in all their misery and woe. Day after day she repeated these visits; night after night she sat, a lonely watcher, by the bedside of some poor creature, sick unto death. A plague has fallen on the city; thousands have been destroyed, but there are thousands, too, who live to bless her name. She has entered the hospital. It is crowded with the sick ones, and

many an eye follows her as she moves from couch to couch.   Suddenly
she stands still as struck with a nameless dread.   Before her lies an old
man, motionless, dying.   Thin gray locks were gathered over his
wrinkled brow, and his pain-furrowed face was flushed with fever.   But
now, as he turns his head, the light of the glorious morning falls on his
wasted features, and he looks once more as in youth.   With a glad cry
of surprise and wonder Evangeline casts herself before him.   " Gabriel,
O my beloved !" she cried, and the dying man smiled sweetly.   Many
the words he strove to utter but every one died on his lips.   She
stooped down and kissed his cold brow.

> " Then sweet was the light of his eyes; but it suddenly sank into darkness
> As when a lamp is blown out by a gust of wind at a casement,
> And as she pressed once more the lifeless head to her bosom
> Meekly she bowed her own, and murmured, ' Father, I thank Thee.' "

Thus ends this great poem, teaching us the beauty and value of hope
and patience; teaching us, too, that these simple qualities, when exercised
with purity of heart, may rise to the height of heroic virtues.

The Smiles of Life.

That line of the poet.

> "Man !"
>
> " Thou pendulum betwixt a smile and tear."

has justly been praised as one of the finest in our language.

Yet, some how or other, it would seem sometimes that we gravitate
towards tears much more frequently than towards smiles.   In the hope,
then, of regulating this pendulum of nature, that it may sway more
evenly, I have sought to present a few thoughts on smiles.

Quintilian tells us that each nation has certain peculiarities which mark out the people of that nation as distinct from all others. But whatever be the customs, howsoever different their dress, how opposed their ways of thought, all agree in this, that they smile when glad.

That smiles and their causes were appreciated by the Romans is clear from the Satires of Horace. For as Blair well says : " He smiles while he reproves." How these Satires must have been enjoyed by the Roman litterateurs of the day, showing us, as they do, the inner life of the people.

The amusing account of the Via Sacra, is toothsome, where the poet encounters the bore of the first magnitude, and after every possible effort to rid himself of this importunate fellow without success, at last puts this question :

> " Have you a father, mother, kin
> " To whom your life is precious ? "
> " None, I've closed the eyes of everyone.
> " Oh, happy they, I inly groan,
> " Now I am left, and I alone."

And the despair of the poet when Fuscus Aristius fails him :—

Ecce—

> Fuscus Aristius occurrit, mihi carus et illum
> Qui pulchre nosset. Consistimus. Unde venis ? Et
> Quo tendis ? rogat et respondet. Vellere coepi,
> Et prensare manu lentissima brachia, nutans,
> Distorquens oculos, ut me eriperet. Male salsus
> Ridens dissimulare.

Imagine, if you can, especially you who have had the pleasure of meeting book canvassers when you had four minutes for your train, imagine, I ask you, how Aristius must have smiled at the plight Horace was in.

Men's smiles are rare ; their tears still more rare. Of woman's tears it has been said that they generally mean nothing. It is needless to contradict this ungallant charge, but treating it with a silent contempt, let us rather consider the rich treasure of her smile.

Shakespeare says :—

> " Those happy smiles that played upon her ripe lip,
> Seem not to know what guests were in her eyes,
> Which parted then as pearls from diamonds dropped,"

While Pope tells us that :

> " Each pleasing Blount shall endless smiles bestow,
> And soft Belindas' blush forever glow."

Happy, indeed, are those whose ways are brightened by the fond smile of a loving mother, a wife, or a fair young maiden, who mirrows forth in herself the grace and virtue of a Beatrice, of Acadia's fair daughter, Evangeline, or of an Elaine.

Even Sir Galahad, the hero whom Arthur loved, knew this.

> " How sweet are looks that ladies bend
> On whom their favors fall ;
> For them I battle to the end
> To save from shame and thrall."

Most truly sang Thomas Campbell when he said :

> " The world was sad, the garden was a wild,
> And man, the hermit, sighed, till woman smiled."

Smiles like all other things are of many varieties.

The child's smile and the matron's, the maiden's radiant features, and the soft, contented smile of gentle old age.

> " Without the smile from partial beauty won,
> O what were man ?—a world without a sun."

And in turn to the maiden fair, what richer reward than the smile of brave and manly affection from her chivalrous hero.

Now of the smile which comes in childhood's happy days. A short time ago I witnessed a very amusing incident which will be a good illustration. I had occasion to pass by a kindergarten one afternoon about the time of dismissal. There was a very young miss, perhaps five years old, coming down the stoop, and on the sidewalk a young gentleman, who, I should judge, was about the same age. When their eyes met, a sort of rosy tinge could be seen gradually flushing their cheeks, and then, as if by one impulse, they thrust their index fingers in their mouths, and on their youthful countenances came

—"a smile that glowed
Celestial rosy red, love's proper hue."

The smile to be most cultivated is the one which brings joy and comfort to the oppressed, or suffering. What a vast difference between the man who, discontented with himself and the world at large, frowns on all, smiles on none, and the gentle, womanly instinct, which ever remembers that

" A smile recures the wounding of a frown."

We have given but a hurried glance at a few of the numerous kinds of smiles, and the ideas they have suggested to the poets. Yet we trust we have made an impression deep enough to show that we should never darken our looks with anger, and if we keep these lines of Milton ever before us, we may be certain of happiness.

Sweet intercourse
Of looks and smiles ; for smiles from reason flow,
To brute denied, and are of man the food.

The Language of Birds.

I AM a curious student of birds. Understand me well. Their plumage everybody can admire. Even a city gamin can probably distinguish a crow from a nightingale. But my studies do not trench upon the sphere of Wilson and Audubon. I commend their most interesting and delightful works to your perusal.

But I have always been persuaded that there was some meaning in birds' voices. When the crow made a noise, insane human beings said, imitatively, "Caw, caw, caw," as if that silly sound disposed of the matter. When the nightingale or the jovial bobolink soared or tumbled, and sang, the same hopeless people said, "Twee, twee, twee," as if birds were natural fools. Now, it early occurred to my mind, as I lay in the meadows and in the woods, that the birds, overhearing the lovely Patti, Scalchi, or Albani, might foolishly say among themselves, "Hear those women going twee, twee, twee." Or if our feathered fellow-creatures should chance to listen to an oration of the Hon. Launcy M. Delew, they might, and, possibly misunderstandingly, declare that the distinguished after-dinner speaker went "Caw, caw, caw."

Here was an evident want of mutual intelligence. Why should men and birds do each other this extremely unnecessary injustice? And I reflected, farther, if we could only establish an understanding, how much might be gained to both sides? How much pleasure to men, if they could only know just the sentiment with which the lark wishes the sun good morning! How much fun to birds if they could only catch the drift of some of our laughter-provoking comedies!

To wish was always with me to act. I devoted myself to study. I spare you the details, and the method I can only communicate upon receipt of a phœnix's egg, blown by an Amazon and filled with Captain

Kidd's buried doubloons.   But the results you shall have—you and the world, for you are both my friends.

I achieved the bird language.   No canary in a cage, no blackbird in the tree, no hen in the barn-yard had any secrets from me longer.   I heard Chanticleer recite his loves to Partlet, and I advise young Damon, the poet, to learn the bird language if he wishes a few hints for lyrical verse.   I heard the greedy refrain of the crow, contemptuous and gross. I heard the sparkling sarcasm of the cat-bird, and the timid talk of the wren.   As for the pigeons, their wooing was so tender that I wished I had wings.   In the deep, dark woods, the thrush poured out a gurgling dithyrambic, to which Anacreon was as dull cider to champagne.   Why should I go on?   You understand I had mastered the mystery, and now, not only their private affairs as hens and wrens, but their great public affairs as birds were laid open to my intelligence.

Now, upon my lawn are several trees.   There is one great elm, and at some distance from it a small cherry tree, and immediately beyond the cherry is a beech.   In August I lay half dozing under the elm, which was filled with blackbirds in great numbers, chatting among themselves. I gathered from what they said, that some of their young had lately set up for themselves in the beech a little colony of blackbirds.   " We must have them in view," said the wise papa blackbirds, " we must look after those little fellows, and be able to fly straight to them when we wish." " Of course, of course," replied the rest, and the great elm over my head murmured with the bird-chorus.   I saw upon the extreme edge of a bough a group of blackbirds chatting very earnestly together.   One of them said that the yellow birds in the cherry tree were quarreling, and one of the parties had asked some of the little colony upon the beech to come over and help them.   So the little blackbirds flew into the cherry tree and fought with some of the yellow birds until all was quiet again, except some sullen yellow birds, who said the blackbirds ought to go home again to the beech.   But these little gentry had found

cherries exceedingly to their taste. "They are truly delicious," they
exclaimed, and they had sent to the elm tree to say that if some more
blackbirds would only fly over they could easily drive out the yellow
birds and have all the cherries to themselves. This proposition was
the subject of much discussion among the little birds upon the bough
over my head. But I heard the great man of birds in the elm declare
that it was not fair, because the yellow birds had the same right to their
little cherry tree that the blackbirds had to the elm and the beech.
Then there was a great wrangling, and I went into dinner.

The next day I went out under the tree and heard the debate again.

I found that many of the birds that I had heard upon the bough
in the elm had flown over to feast upon the cherries, and a great
many others wanted to go. But the poor little yellow birds were
fluttering about, and summoning all who would come—the wrens, and
sparrows, and tom-tits, and other small feathered fry, and they were
alighting upon the tips of the boughs on which sat the naughty little
black buccaneers. Dinner was very early this day, so I heard no more;
but when I came out, some time afterward, it appeared that the yellow
birds, with their little allies, had gradually descended from the boughs
on which they had alighted and driven the blackbirds toward the end
of one great bough to which they clung.

Then these last sent messages to the elm, and said to the papa blackbirds that they must come and help them, or they should be driven out
of the cherry tree, and if they were, it would be much farther to fly
round the cherry to the beech. So the old elm tree was noisy enough
with the chattering of the birds. "Let us fly to their rescue!" cried
one very young and very black bird. "Why should we see our own
color and species driven out of a good cherry tree? The blackbirds
have a natural right to cherries." "Pooh!" interrupted an older one;
"yellow birds have just as much right to the fruit as we have, and they
were there first. Let them be, and eat their own cherries. In all con-

science *we* have enough." "That may be," broke in another of the fiery young ones; "but we want a shorter cut to the beech tree this hot weather. We must go through the cherry tree, where we can rest in the shade, and solace our little stomachs. Come on ! who is for the cherry tree !" "Fiddle !" replied a grizzly old bird; "its both shorter and easier to fly round the cherry tree than to go through it. You little silly birds, you disgrace the name of blackbird." "That's all very well," said one, "but it is the inevitable destiny of blackbirds to overspread all cherry trees, and why should you resist the design of nature ?"

The elm fairly shook with the tempest of applause that followed this speech, and Launcy Delew Blackbird, Esquire, resumed his perch with the air of a bird who has picked the cherry stone clean. "It's no more the design of nature," said old grizzle, "than it is that every blackbird shall be shot by truant boys. Truant boys are bigger and can shoot, but they've no business to be playing truant, and they've no right to shoot us merely because we can't shoot back again." There was no denying the truth of this, and finding all the other birds to be silent, old grizzle continued: "Besides if you think the ability is the argument, you have only to see that the yellow birds have been able to drive out the naughty little blackbirds, or to hem them in; and so according to your own argument, the time has not yet arrived for the occupation of that particular cherry tree."

Old grizzle hopped to his perch, and I could hear the most confused bawling as to the true policy to pursue. But when I last looked at the cherry tree, a few forlorn blackbirds, who had evidently eaten no cherries for a long, long time, were fluttering feebly among the boughs, while crowds of fat little yellow birds were chirping songs of defiance, and putting their bills and claws into them without mercy.

Thus the trees are full of birds who are waging these funny little contests all the time. I have not yet investigated the intercourse of fish, but I have no doubt I should find the same thing going on in the

water as in the air.   The result of my bird-knowledge, gathered from
a hundred episodes like the one I send you, is a satisfaction with my
species, and a calm delight that men are not as blackbirds are.

The Story of Esther.

'Tis bridal festival and banquet night
In King Assuerus' glittering palace court;
High on his throne hung with green canopy
And set with heavy tapestry of gold,
Looped with its purple silken cords in rings
Of ivory, he stood, the monarch lord
Of India to the Ethiopian shore.

With peerless mien, and clad in priceless robes,
There sat the fair Queen Esther at his side;
Bright flashed the gems and jewels of her crown
That lurked amid her perfumed tresséd hair.
Each Mede and haughty Persian envied him
For she was first among the flattering fair,
Her glancing eye, her grace so won them all.

The revelry is done, the wine is quaffed,
The torches in the banquet hall are dimmed,
The gentle patter of the sandal hushed;
And onward home proceed the beauteous train,
Each youth in joy, each maid in ecstacy,
Shaking the midnight dewdrop from the rose;
So hies the queen unto the sleeping hall.

She threw her robe and veil upon the couch,
And placed aside her ruby-studded crown;
Then lit the taper, and the incense urn,
And took the drooping tulip from her breast,
Undid the pearls about her queenly neck;
And thus with eyes upturned and hand outstretched,
She knelt upon the marble floor in prayer,

"O Esther!" cried a voice—her curtains moved
And Mordechai, her uncle, who had watched
Her when an orphan child in Babylon,
Stood there: " O spare thine uncle and thy race!
I saved thy king, but now through Aman's fraud
And envy, on the gibbet I shall die."
He sped—and left her there in fear to pray:

" My Lord, my God! they oft had said that Thou
Wouldst choose among the nations, Israel:
But in Thy sight we've sinned, and now Thou hast
Delivered us into a hostile hand;
Thou knowest, Lord, my country well I love,
Then deign to give my tongue a charm of speech
That I may calm the king's fierce hardened heart."

Next morn she dressed in fairest gown, and saw
The king—he knit his brow—no courtier dared
Approach his throne unless the favored called;
She trembled like the timid doe—but God
Had moved the king—he took her by the hand
And cried: What wouldst thou say? for thou shalt have,
If half my mighty kingdom it shall be."

She said : " My lord, I am a Jewess born,
My uncle, Mordechai, the Jew who saved
Thee from the plot to slay thy majesty
Is now condemned ; thy courtier Aman, whom
Thou lov'st, is false to thee, and has decreed
' Each Jew shall die ;' as humble wife I pray
My loving husband, king, to let them live."

Each courtier, dusky slave and servant shout :
" 'Tis true, he is a traitor, base and false !"
In wrath the angry king his garden paced,
Then rushing in, he stood upon his throne
And spoke : " 'Tis sad, but Aman thou shalt die !"
Then looking tenderly upon the queen,
He gently said : " Thy people shall be spared."

"The Way It Happened."

IN YOUR mind fashion a boy of medium height, with dark features and
hair and eyes to match ; straight and slender in form, and about
eighteen years old, and you will identify him as no other than Joe
Clancy. His frank face and noble bearing will impress you as belonging to one who would not stoop to do a base act. Good nature shines
from his dark eyes, while his broad shoulders, expanded chest and
hard muscles exhibit thorough athletic training. In his own way Joe
was an athlete. That is, he had grasped and profited by whatever ad-
vantages were held forth by the small gymnasium attached to the school
he attended, and, by constant practice, had acquired a constitution and
form often admired by his companions. But the gymnasium did not
bound his world of athletic pursuits. Games and sports in the open

air charmed him. He gloried in base-ball in the summer ; in autumn, the opposing team, with reasons, feared his skill in foot-ball ; on the ponds in winter, he was the fleetest, and most graceful skater ; on the hills, the most daring coaster. Then, at school, though not the brightest boy in his class, his rank was by no means lowly.

But all that he cultivated—a manly form, robust health, and considerable knowledge—he intended to use when, if ever, the hope of his life were realized. He aimed to enter the military academy at West Point and to graduate from there a soldier, possibly a general. Alas, for his fond hopes ! Among all his friends there was not one with influence sufficient to instal him at West Point. Still, in spite of this, and although as he grew older, his hopes assumed a Utopian appearance, he manfully struggled to brighten his darkening prospects.

Joe had two brothers, George and Jim, both younger than himself. They resembled him in all his habits and inclinations save this, that they were averse to following a military career. Ridicule after ridicule they heaped upon Joe for the zeal with which he strove to reach so impossible a goal. Although their unkind cuts vexed him, they in no manner weakened his efforts, for in a short time he purchased a rifle and, by constant practice, became an expert marksman.

The season for foot-ball was now at hand. Numerous teams popped up wherever eleven could be found. Victory savored defeat, and the rivalry became more intense the nearer the end of the season approached. Joe's team was called the " Dreadnaughts." Indeed, it can be truly called " Joe's team." Through his efforts it was formed ; under his management it improved in strength year by year, until its name truly characterized its nature. It did not fear any opponent, but there was one club, the " Conquerors," to defeat which it was necessary for the Dreadnaughts to use all available strength and strategy, and even then the Conquerors sometimes won.

Toward the close of the season, all other teams had been defeated, and the final struggle was with these two rivals. Six of the seven games between them had already been contested. Three Dreadnaught victories and an equal number for the Conquerors was the result. What a desperate struggle was the seventh ! On a level soil, grassy and springy, the opposing elevens faced each other. Joe encouraged his companions, pointing out to them the seeming weaknesses of their opponents, and devising tricks to overcome their strength. With both sides inflamed with the determination of victory, the struggle began.

I will not describe it. You know too well how, fearing defeat and yearning for victory, the contestants throw aside all care and recklessly encounter dangers. Thought for life or limb seems to have deserted them. So it was with Joe. He fought with Herculean efforts in a desperate scrimmage, captured the ball, and, hotly pressed, bore it to the right point and with one line kick scored a Dreadnaught victory.

Victory, then, at least, was sweet, but an enormous price purchased it. In that dreadful scrimmage, Joe's left arm was doubly fractured. A stinging pain first announced the unfortunate accident. Rather than succumb to his rivals, and thus to dishearten his comrades, he bore with it. Poor fellow ! Winter was just beginning. Skating and coasting, his particular delights, were excellent. Alas for him ! he wished that neither snow nor ice was ever known in these parts. From his home he would hear the joyful voices of the coasters, mingled with the blasts of the course horn. From the front window, the scene of a lake of ice with revelling skaters skimming over its glassy surface, lay open before his longing eyes. Often he wished to tear the bandages from his arm and share in these scenes of enjoyment. Often he sought to deafen his ears to this jollity by sleep. But the thought of his lost enjoyment preyed on his mind, and the days dragged slowly along.

For two months Joe suffered as though imprisoned. At the end of that time, an attending doctor, a man who became most attached to his patient and encouraged his hopes for West Point, allowed him to coast. This privilege was joyfully received, although Joe was enjoined to abandon all thoughts of skating.

Winter's last traces had faded, and spring's gentle hand to be felt in the soft zephyrs, when Joe's disabled arm had returned to its former self. As I have said before there was, at a little distance from his home, a large lake, on whose placid bosom, rested the boats moored there by their owners. Among them Joe had his boat—built for speed, long and with a narrow beam. Daily and almost nightly, the proud owner of the craft glided noiselessly through the peaceful waters, now moving with measured dips, and again speeding in friendly rivalry with his comrades.

One evening, when the stars overhead twinkled, and the moon illumined the surface of the water, carrying the oars on his shoulder, Joe sought his boat. The lake was lined with rowers, and the shore lined with strollers. Soon Joe was in the middle of the lake, and as he quietly sailed along, chatted with a schoolmate.

" Joe, I think this night was made for us," said his friend.

" Well, if it was, it couldn't be made more perfect. Everybody takes advantage of it, too. Say, Phil, what do you think of forming a boat-club around here?" asked Joe.

" Capital idea ! What put that into your head ?"

" Why," answered Joe, "there is not a—"

Suddenly the still air was rent with an appealing cry " Help ! Help !"

Joe abruptly ceased, and excitedly scanned the waters. About two hundred yards up the lake he saw an overturned boat. Near it a dress was slowly sinking. Instantly he turned his boat, and with his mighty strength, pulled to the rescue. Again rose the pleading cry, now faintly, " Help ! He—!"—but the cruel waters closed over her and cut off her agonizing appeal. The speed of the boat is redoubled. Nearer to the drowning one it glides. For the third time a piteous face appears on the surface, and then out from his boat and into the waters plunges the noble rescuer.   Below the water sinks the gasping woman, with her eyes turned appealingly towards him.   In a moment she reappears supported by the daring boy.

The other craft had now crowded about, attracted by the commotion, and the lady was lifted in an insensible state from the water.   Joe climbed into his boat and soon was bound homeward for a dry outfit. A few days erased all thought of the incident from his mind.   However, before a week had passed, a letter addressed to " Mr. Joseph Clancy," and bearing the seal of William Lewis, Congressman, awakened his interest.   This is the letter.

Dear Sir :

The invaluable service you have rendered to my family shall be indelibly stamped on my memory.   All my earthly possessions would be but a slight mark of my gratitude.   Accept the enclosed commission for West Point, not as a recompense, but as a token that for the rest of my life I shall ever bless you for this inestimable favor.

Your true friend,   WILLIAM LEWIS.

This is how it came about.   The young lady whom Joe had rescued was the daughter of this Congressman, and in her convalescence was attended by the same physician that doctored Joe's arm.   The loving father, eager to show his gratitude, consulted the physician, and he, well knowing Joe's craving to enter West Point, advised Mr. Lewis accordingly.   The result was the letter and commission, and shortly after Joe assumed the military uniform.

" White with the Years of the Altar."

White with the years of the altar,
  With half a century's snows,
White with the unceasing conflict
  Waged 'gainst the Holy One's foes.
All hail to the Prince of the faithful,
  Hail to the Prince of God ;
Hail to the grand mitred hero
  White with the years of the Lord.

The gems of thy crowning tiara
  Gleam in their lustre bright,
Breathing a soft, sweet story
  Unto the bright rays of light ;
A story falling softer than snowflakes
  Shrouding the whispering night.

And the tale of their jeweled telling,
  Waking the sweet echoes there,
Sped on its way to the altar,
  Softer than soft-whispered prayer.
Telling the tale of a lifetime,
  The tale of a God-serving life,
Serving in cloistered quiet
  And serving 'mid years of strife.

Lo ! in the far distant gloaming,
  Of the dim, half-forgotten past,
While a ray of the coming glory
  O'er his young life was cast,
He pledged himself in the springtime
  Of his youth and his strength to God,
And became of the chosen captains
  In the army of the Lord.

He raised the holy chalice
   In the holy Mass each day,
While the precious years of his youth-time
   Were silently slipping away;
But the golden after-promise
   Shone with a far brighter ray.

And sometimes in noblest verses,
   He sang as the poet's sang;
And after his daily toiling
   Their melody sweetly rang;
As after their toils of the daytime,
   The breath of the fresh summer night
Is sweeter to weary mortals
   Than aught save the first break of light.

Lo! And a far nobler day break,
   A fuller, more perfect dawn,
Breaks on the white-crowned lifetime
   And grows to a glorious morn.
'Tis a decade, but one more white blossom
   Of service, encrowning his brow,
But ten of the short and e'er fleeting
   Years from the e'er fleeting now.

When seething, the giant sea-waves
   Raged, as they would overwhelm
Christ's bark, a steady pilot
   Took the tempest-tost helm,
And Leo was chose in the choosing
   As Prince of a heavenly realm.

As Prince of uncounted battalions,
   Unnumbered as sands on the shore,
And far from the East and the West now
   Rolls their acclaiming roar,

Pealing in saint-sung " Te Deums,"
 Hailing the chosen of heaven.
And back from the sunburst of promise
 The dark mists of doubt are now driven.

Oh Thou, that leadest Thy children,
 Great is Thy glory grown,
For never a princelier ruler
 Sat on that martyr-pressed throne.
For lo! he who boasted of conquest,
 And was strong in the blood-glutted sword,
The man of blood and of iron,
 Bowed to the man of God.

Great is thy glory, O Leo,
 Great, but a greater is here
Won thee, by ceaseless endeavor,
 By toil, thro' each lingering year
Of thy youth and the prime of thy manhood,
 And in age now, the crowning is near.

It is come; the white coronet's gathered
 And shines o'er thy noble brow,
And the grace of thy fifty years' priesthood
 Doth crown thee with happiness now.
Tho' the years may lie heavy upon thee,
 Yet strong is thy will, as of old,
And thy long years of work have but proved thee,
 As trying doth chasten the gold.

Fifty long years Christ's sentinel,
 Thro' a Jubilee found at thy post,
While the song of each dead day's upraising
· Still sang thee as watching the host

E'er faithful thro' morning and noontide,
     And now in the shadows of eve,
What a halo of well won glory
     Shall the set of the sun round thee weave!

Thou hero! thy western battalions,
     Massed in this land of the free,
Hail thee with loyal devotion,
     And over the deep-ridged sea,
The song of their soldierly welcome
     Is borne by the winds unto thee!

And we in our still younger legion,—
     Young, but with hearts full as bold
For thee, and with service as loyal
     As any, whose praises have rolled
Over the land and the ocean—
     Hail thee as Prince of our race,
As strong as ever man in thy wisdom
     And stronger than man in thy grace.

The Gleam of the Golden Leaf.

The gentle shepherd's heart was sad; his pipe
Was mute and silent in pure sympathy.
"Dark, dreary is the dismal earth," said he.
"The woods, the meads all frown, the streams run by,
Nor greet me with their tinkling tunes of yore.
Ah, surely, surely nature is in pain,
I'll hie me to the woods and pipe a strain
To gladness bring to all. Now to the woods."
He went, and 'neath a spicy fir he sate,
Then 'tween his lips the oaten reed he placed,

And soft at first, the strains the stillness chased,
Then softly, gently grew the plaintive tune.
Now dies the music, and the notes are low.
The woodland elves and dryads from the shades
In wonder gather round.   The forest glades
With listful, silent nymphs and satyrs fill.
Now flow the liquid tones in melody
So strong, so soft, so sad, the forests round
Are silent, and the winds low moaning sound
Into a whisper dies.   The very leaves,
That fretful on the branches trembled wild, ·
Are still and awed, as breaks the limpid strain
In flights of sound and then returns again,
For nature is within the shepherd's charm.
Then casts he down his slender pipe and stands
And to the listening crowd he bears his song.
About him eagerly now pressed that throng
With ears intent to hear the coming lay.
" Ye woodland elves no more do ye rejoice,
Ye forest dryads, satyrs, nymphs of fount
And mead and hill and dale, why are ye sad?
Ye brooks, why list ? ye answer not my song?
Ye woods, ye forests, what is't that is wrong?
In gloom ye all are rapt.   Joy is no more.
What wails the winds among the sighing limbs?
Why sigh those limbs ?   What whisper e'er the leaves ?
O answer nature's children, answer me."
Now does the moaning of the trees begin ;
Now wails the wind, now sighs the grassy mead.
Hark ! Now the winds the woeful answer leads,
"Woe! woe! Sweet Summer's gone; dear Summer's dead,"
And nymphs and elfin folk and brook and mead,
And woodland dryads, timorous bird and hare
The wail begins and sighing fill the air.

The trees their arms to Heav'n in sorrow wave;
And dark the vault above in pity grows.
"Fair Summer's dead! Our Summer's dead! she's dead!
And parted from us ever, now," they said.
Then 'gan the shepherd's eyes to brighter grow.
"Take heart, fair Summer lives; she is not dead,
She is but sleeping, resting now," he said.
The group around, half doubting, full of joy,
In new-born gladness broke the silence long.
"Dear Summer is not dead; she sleeps at rest.
Why are we in these mournful garments drest?
Why mourn we? rise! rejoice! rejoice!"
Then skipped the merry forest folk in joy;
Then sang a merry strain the joyful brook,
And every hill and dell and every nook
In brightness grew; and gladness filled the earth.
"Let's don the purple royal," said the trees,
"Let's cast aside our sober gowns again,"
And see! mead, forest, wood and copse and glen
In one harmonious burst of color glow.
The shepherd started.   Grief was gone e'er more.
His merry pipe a tripping measure trilled.
The earth and sky around with joy was filled.
"Summer will come! she sleeps, she is not dead."

Vulcan's Thunder.

I HAD been studying ancient mythology for some hours one winter's night, when the clock striking one, caused me to look up. "11:30, and not done yet," I thought wearily. I went to the window, raised the sash and looked out. Snow had been falling since 5 o'clock and it was now thick on the street. The passers-by made no noise as they walked; no wagons rolled heavily along; and, but for the toot of the tin horns in the hands of some impatient youngsters, all was still. Yes, everything and everyone was saving his strength to take part in the mighty tornado of sound which, in half an hour, was to usher in another year. "So," thought I, "this year was welcomed at its advent, but now, as ever, they turn to welcome the new-comer and leave the present to die unheeded.

Well, such is life. I closed the window and returned to the fire-place with a shiver, sat down, put my feet on the fender, took my myth-ology, and began to study. I had twenty-five minutes for study, as it would be impossible to learn anything while the din lasted. After hav-ing learned some lines I closed my eyes to recite, in order to make sure that I knew them. But in less than two minutes I was far from the fireside and discoursing on the gods of antiquity. Of Vulcan I spoke with greatest force—told of his position in heaven, his misfortunes, his generosity in making helmets, shields and thunderbolts gratis,—I gave forth ideas beyond the power of man to grasp, with words so enr4ptur-ing that no silver-tongued orator ever yet has equalled them. Ah! what now remains of that speech? Not a word; not even a thought. For immortal though I seemed to be, I was but human. Becoming fatigued I asked for a glass of water, which I drank; and instantly subject, audi-ence, applause, yea, even myself had disappeared. I was again removed and seemingly borne along through space, back to the time when, six years of age, upon my return from school, I used to fling my shoes and stockings in at the door and run off to enjoy my stolen freedom, wholly forgetting the mercilous "cat-o'nine-tails" which hung on the wall, impatiently awaiting my return at dark.

There I stood, at the door of the old blacksmith shop. There was old Faber Ferrarius, griping in his strong hand a large pair of iron pincers, which held a red-hot piece of iron that he and his assistant, Billy, rapped alternately with large, heavy hammers. How strange it all was! Surely it was some years since I had been there before, yet nothing had changed. The same pair of spectacles sat complacently on the old man's large Roman nose. Billy was no older, and he had on the same red flannel shirt. On the rafters hung different sized shoes as they always had done. The same two forges stood on the west side of the room. Still I felt that at some time I had been older and taller. However, I was assured that everything was as it should be, when, the iron becoming cold, good old Ferrarius again stuck it into the fire and turning around caught sight of me. "Hello, little fellow," he said, "you were kept in at school to-day." I was going to say that I stayed in to make a speech, but then my thoughts became so confused I couldn't say anything. But I soon recovered, and before the iron was hot I was chatting away with the two artisans.

Now the metal was again hot. Ferrarius drew it out and brought it to the anvil. Then I noticed for the first time that he found it difficult to lift his feet as he walked. The hammering began. Such a noise! It nearly deafened me. Yet these mechanics talked as quietly as if there was no other sound than their own voices. But, strange to say, I caught what was said only after the hammering ceased. It was Billy who spoke. "Vulcan," said he, "I think we need some more coal, I'll go and *fire up*." While he was "firing up," the blacksmith began to sing. When he had finished I asked him for a horse-shoe nail. "What do you want with a horse-shoe nail? I didn't like to tell him that I wanted it to scratch my name on the desk, as Jimmy Thompson had done with his jack-knife. How I envied that jack-knife! After a little more questioning, however, he gave me one as long as myself, with a large, hammered head, on which it would stand when I set it down. "Hurry up with your coal, Cyclops," shouted Vulcan, "this bolt must be done very soon."

I was greatly puzzled to know if Vulcan had given up the horse-shoeing business, and gone into the manufacture of hardware. But I was glad to learn Billy's last name, for I never had heard it before. So when he made his appearance with a large scuttle of coal, I shouted: "Hello, Billy Cyclops! See what Vulcan gave me," holding up the over-grown horse-shoe nail. "I suppose you will steal an apple from every grocery store you pass now," he said. I looked up into his face to see if he meant what he said, and to my surprise I saw that he had but one eye. "Oh! Billy," I asked, "where is your other eye?" He told me that a spark had struck it and injured it so that it had to be taken out, and that the doctor had moved the other to the middle of his forehead for the sake of harmony.

Vulcan drew out the bolt, which was now about four feet long and a foot in diameter. His object seemed now to be to force the end of this hollow cylinder into a large iron cap, with a nicely-shaped steel handle on it. They began to hammer. The noise was awful. A shower of sparks spurted in all directions, and I thought that most of them must have been struck against my bare shins. I was glad to get out of the way by going to the door of the smithy, where a crowd of children and a blue-coated policeman stood, watching the operation.

When the smith and his one-eyed attendant had succeeded in forcing the cap over the end, Vulcan again threw it into the fire, saying to Billy: "Now, Cyclops, get the other cap and the bolt will be complete." Cyclops started to obey. Before doing so, however, he went to the door and ordered the crowd of children to disperse. Only one or two left the place, and as he was in a hurry he did not wait to enforce the command, but went to get the iron cap. I went in again and accosted the smith with: "What do they use that for?" "That's what makes the thunder," he replied. While he was speaking, the policeman came into the room, jumped in after the bolt and was soon covered with coal. "How does that make the thunder?" I asked, not in the least surprised by this strange act. "Why, you see," he began with equal complacency, "there's a handle at each end. One takes a hold of one, another of the other; and they push them along—that makes the thunder. Now when two run against each other, they come together pretty hard and explode—that makes the lightning. D'ye see? When there's what they call a good big thunder-storm, they use up about a hundred or a hundred and fifty of these bolts."

I would have asked him how much it costs for a good big thunder storm, but I was prevented by the policeman emerging from the fire and walking out to the middle of the floor, shaking the sparks from him and the whole building with each step. The other children ran away scared at the sight. I could hear them call me, but I was surprised that I could not stir. Far as I was from him I could feel the heat, for this strange being was almost one mass of fire. As he advanced towards me I felt the warmth of the place uncomfortable in proportion, and, having dispensed with shoes and stockings, my uncovered legs suffered most. He advanced till he stood beside me. I could not move. He seized me and then I started, struggled, kicked, shouted—in vain. I threw back my head to catch a glance of Billy Cyclops. His one eye shone directly in mine. The brazen-faced man seemed to be hissing with heat; I was shouting, Vulcan was hammering his bolt with his big heavy sledge, yet, above all the noise and din, I could hear a clear vibration as if the anvil rang with each blow on the bolt, ding, ding, ding. I awoke. At a glance I understood that it was the clock striking five. I had been dreaming; my head having been thrown back, the lamp shone in my half-opened eyes; my foot had slipped over the fender and had deposited itself under the grate, and was being warmed to such a degree as to be likely to cause serious damage. I jumped up, and as I glanced at the clock the ringing continued: ding, ding. "Here it is five o'clock in the morning," I thought. A banging at the door attracted my attention in that direction. I opened it and "A Happy New Year" greeted my ears from one who had come to spend with me the holidays of the New Year.

The Story Of A Drama.

IF IT were left to mere conjecture to account for the origin of the drama, one might very naturally suppose that it naturally arose from what appears to be an innate propensity in man, to take an interest in and to recount the sayings and doings of others. Even among the cultivated classes of the present day—and far more so is it the case among the uncultivated and uneducated, who are living examples of what all classes at one time were—when two or three meet together, are not the affairs of themselves and their friends, almost invariably, the staple subject of conversation? And if any one with his ears open passes two gossips in conversation, he is almost sure to observe that the one is recounting to the other, in an animated and dramatic manner, some exploit of which he or she is the victorious hero or heroine. In this way, however, the origin of the epic would perhaps be more appropriately accounted for, it being essentially a narrative set forth by one narrator, generally interspersed with fragments of conversation, and resembling the drama in being concerned with the exhibition of a progressive action. The epic, I believe, was the first form of poetry, if not of all literature, and at first was probably nothing more than mere narrative vigorously and picturesquely set forth. We can not fail to see its striking resemblance to the drama, and one's fancy would instantly suggest them to have taken their origin from the same source.

Theoretically, however, to account for the origin of the drama, in addition to the gossipping or story-telling propensity in man, we have also to take into consideration the earliest developed and perhaps the strongest of all his propensities—that of imitation or mimicry. This propensity is seen in earliest childhood ; without it there would be no possibility of education. Are not the very games of children merely the mimicry of the serious life-business of their elders ? Savages have been described as the children of nature ; and they do resemble children in many respects, especially in the nature of their amusements, which are generally mere imitations or representations of their most serious employments, namely, war and the chase. Among nearly every known people on the face of the globe, from the ultra civilized and theatre-loving Parisian down to the almost brute-like Australian, there is something to be found corresponding to dramatic representation.

Doubtless, in many instances, among savage nations, this takes a very rude form ; but even in its rudest form, it is an outcome of the same propensity as the most elaborate production of the greatest dramatist, namely, a desire to afford pleasure by representing the realities of active life. In its rudest form, it is to be seen in the war-dance of the North American Indians and other savages, which is simply a representation of a battle, and may be regarded as tragedy in its crudest form ; while the comic and love dances of the South Sea Islanders and others exhibit comedy in its earliest stage. Indeed, dancing seems at all times to have been intimately connected with dramatic representation, and one of the most important parts of the ancient drama, the chorus, takes its name from this fact. The great difference in form between the ancient Greek or classic drama and the modern English or romantic drama, is, that in the former was introduced the chorus, which from the part it played originally at the festivals of Bacchus, gradually came to be regarded as an altogether subordinate part of the main drama.

This chorus consisted of a group of persons, in some way connected with the " dramatis personae " who at intervals in the progress of the drama, gave utterance to certain moral reflections, suggested by the scenes, or were used by the dramatist as a means of letting the audience know any details that were necessary to the full understanding of the plot. Only one other difference between the classic and modern or romantic drama can I mention here ; it is, that the former generally endeavored to adhere rigidly to what are known as the dramatic unities of time, place and action. The first of these enacts that to keep up the illusion, everything represented in the drama should happen on the same day ; the second, that for the same reason, all the actions should take place on the same spot, or nearly so ; and the third, that there should be only one main action or plot to which everything else must be subservient. Hence the severity and simplicity of the Greek tragedy, which excluded everything foreign or unnecessary to the subject.

The religious festivals of Bacchus were believed to have been introduced into Greece by Melampus. In the Bacchic ritual an ode in honor of the God was recited ; and to write the ode which would be selected by the priests for their ceremony, became a favorite contest among the poets of the time. A goat was either the principal sacrifice at the altar or the prize awarded to the successful competitor ; thus from the two words, τράγος and ῳδή the ode for the goat, came the Greek word, τραγῳδία tragedy.

Chorus, in Greek, literally means a dance or company of dancers ; and this tragic chorus continued to chant the sorrows and mishaps of Bacchus, as the God of nature in his struggle for life with the adverse powers of winter—hence the meaning which came to be attached to the words tragic and tragedy, for it was from this particular part of the worship of Bacchus that tragedy was developed   As I am not writing a history of the Greek drama, nor even of the drama in general, but have introduced the above statements only because I deemed it necessary to lay before the reader what is known of the origin of the European drama, I will now fulfil my original intention of giving an account of one of Shakespeare's grandest tragedies. Not only did William Shakespeare give to the world grander intellectual brain product than any human being that ever lived, but he passed through life with an harmonious propriety of circumstances and completeness of achievement allotted to few. Born in a lovely English village, bred in wholesome pursuits, physical and intellectual, dwelling amid rural sights and influences during childhood and transplanted to an atmosphere of refinement and accomplishment in London, when just of an age to receive most advantageously this crowning polish, the natural poet became the consummate poet. He retained an affectionate regard for home ties amid the fascinations of town attachments ; he fulfilled his duties of son, brother and father with consistency and truth ; he received public favor ; he won the love of brother-poets and brother-actors ; he secured the admiring esteem and friendship of distinguished noblemen, and he gained the favor of both sovereigns who occupied the English throne during his lifetime. He was held in such high veneration by his own fellow townsmen, that they laid his honored bones close to the very communion-rails of their church, and erected his monumental effigy within the walls of their chancel ; loved as a friend and genial companion by them when alive, reverenced as an ornament to their community in his memory after death.

In one of the Italian novels to which Shakespeare frequently had recourse for his fable, he had the good fortune to meet with the simple and pathetic story of Romeo and Juliet. What he found he has arranged with great skill, and no one of his plays is more frequently represented or honored with more tears. We have in the drama, as a background in harmony with the idea of the whole, the hostile relations of the families of the Montagues and Capulets in the beautiful city of Verona. Then there appear as secondary personages, the worthy Prince Escabus and his military suite, the two heads of the families at feud, and their consorts as well as their immediate servants, Abraham and Balthasar on the Montague side (Romeo's), and Samson, Gregory and Peter on the side of the Capulets. Male and female relations and acquaintances of the two families, citizens of Verona, watchmen, musicians, and similar secondary figures come in naturally, in order to present manifold motley scenes in the life of a great city. It was given to Shakespeare to draw out all this from the theme itself.

Upon this back ground the mournful and lovely history of Romeo Montague and Juliet Capulet passes before us. The foreground of the whole is filled with several chief incidents of their love. Romeo's first meeting at the ball, their marriage, their heroic struggle against the hostile relations of their families, the bliss and the woe of their parting, and finally the reunion in death. It is most wonderful, in what a masterly way the poet has used all the artistic material at his disposal in the treatment of these prominent scenes. Let us look at the work more closely. These two personages, of course, are the chief characters ; with them certain individuals are so connected as subordinate characters that they appear as chief persons of secondary light, not so important as Romeo and Juliet themselves, but coming very prominently forward from the background.

And here it is that a fine trait of the poet appears, that he places at the side of Romeo as the man's two friends, the good Benvolio and the humorist Mercutio, but at the side of Juliet her family—father, mother and cousins, and that great prattler, the droll nurse. Accordingly, old Capulet and Lady Capulet are far more conspicuous than old Montague, Romeo's father and Lady Montague, his mother. Among Juliet's relatives, her cousin Tybalt appears most prominently in the foreground as the fiercest bully of them all, as the hate of the two houses personified. "This butcher of the silk button," as Mercutio calls him, is the character through whom the tragical catastrophe is brought about. But among these subordinate characters Friar Lawrence occupies quite a peculiar position. It is worthy of note that such a benevolent Franciscan friar is a standing figure in the Italian novels, and is intimately associated with Italian life. But Shakespeare has idealized the character. In his hands the good Italian monk becomes a large-minded man, a wise natural philosopher, a shrewd politician, who, in the full freedom of an enlightened mind, stands high above the turmoil of the passions and gives his help to the worthiest aims.

Friar Lawrence represents, as it were, the part of the chorus in this tragedy; when he speaks, we seem to hear the reflections which the poet is making aloud to himself as the play comes from his creative hands. Under the garb of the monk, Shakespeare communicates to us the results of his personal experience, and the conclusions to which the spectacle of the world has led him. He was profoundly versed in the study of human nature ; he knew its weaknesses, its contradictions, its impatient desires and its rashness ; yet the knowledge never lessens his indulgence or his sympathy for his fellow creatures. He smiles at their folly, he is vexed at their weaknesses, and he sometimes sternly summons them back to their duties; but, all the while, he is full of compassion, extending the helping hand, and by wise counsels endeavoring to soften their lot. No longer is he young or passionate like them, but he loves youth, he excuses error, and like the village preacher, his heart always generous, promptly espouses the cause of those whom his reason condemns.

Among all these closely-connected persons, Count Paris stands somewhat isolated. He is the husband-elect of Juliet in a "marriage of convenience," graceful, refined, highly-esteemed, but without the fascinating power of true, manly love. Accordingly the contrast he presents to the enthusiasm of Romeo, heightens the beauty of true love in comparison with the repulsiveness of a marriage forced upon a bride by conventional laws.

Just before Romeo appears and when we know him only by name, the language takes a melodious-poetic character, which, in the most graceful manner possible, brings us a grateful relief from the preceding din of tongues and clash of swords. We become acquainted with him as an inexperienced youth, whose heart glows for Rosaline, one who neither returns nor understands his affection. That Romeo's love for Rosaline is no mere boyish fancy, but a strong, ardent feeling, the poet clearly intimates. Romeo held his beloved Rosaline for the glory of her sex, because he knows no other, and has had no opportunity for comparisons. His sympathizing friend, Benvolio, seeks to give him such an opportunity, because thereby he sees the best way to lead Romeo's affections into the right path. At Benvolio's suggestion, Romeo goes for the first time into a great company, the ball at old Capulet's, and, not to be known, the friends go masked ; he sees Juliet, the daughter of the hostile house, who, like Romeo, appears in such a festal gathering for the first time. Scarcely grown out of child's shoes, but fourteen years of age, freshly blooming human flower, she is destined by her parents to become the wife of the young Count Paris, whom she does not know and has never even seen. . . . . .

The talk of the two friends in the still night is so full of sweet magic, and one is so carried away by it that he can hardly say to himself : "This bliss is too great to find room on earth ; for such overpowering happiness this world of care is not made." . . "Omnia vincit amor," says the poet, and he makes the calm, moderate wisdom of Father Lawrence give way to the ardor of Romeo, not the reverse. Indeed, could we for a moment imagine the intense affection of the young lovers changed or cooled by the persuasive breath of the friar's life, our interest in Romeo and Juliet would be extinguished instantly. But it is increased when the friar gives the benediction of the church to the tie woven by the purest and noblest love.

With Friar Lawrence we foresee that the lovers will be conquered by fate. Shakespeare does not close the tomb upon them until he has crowned them with all the passing, worldly happiness that can be

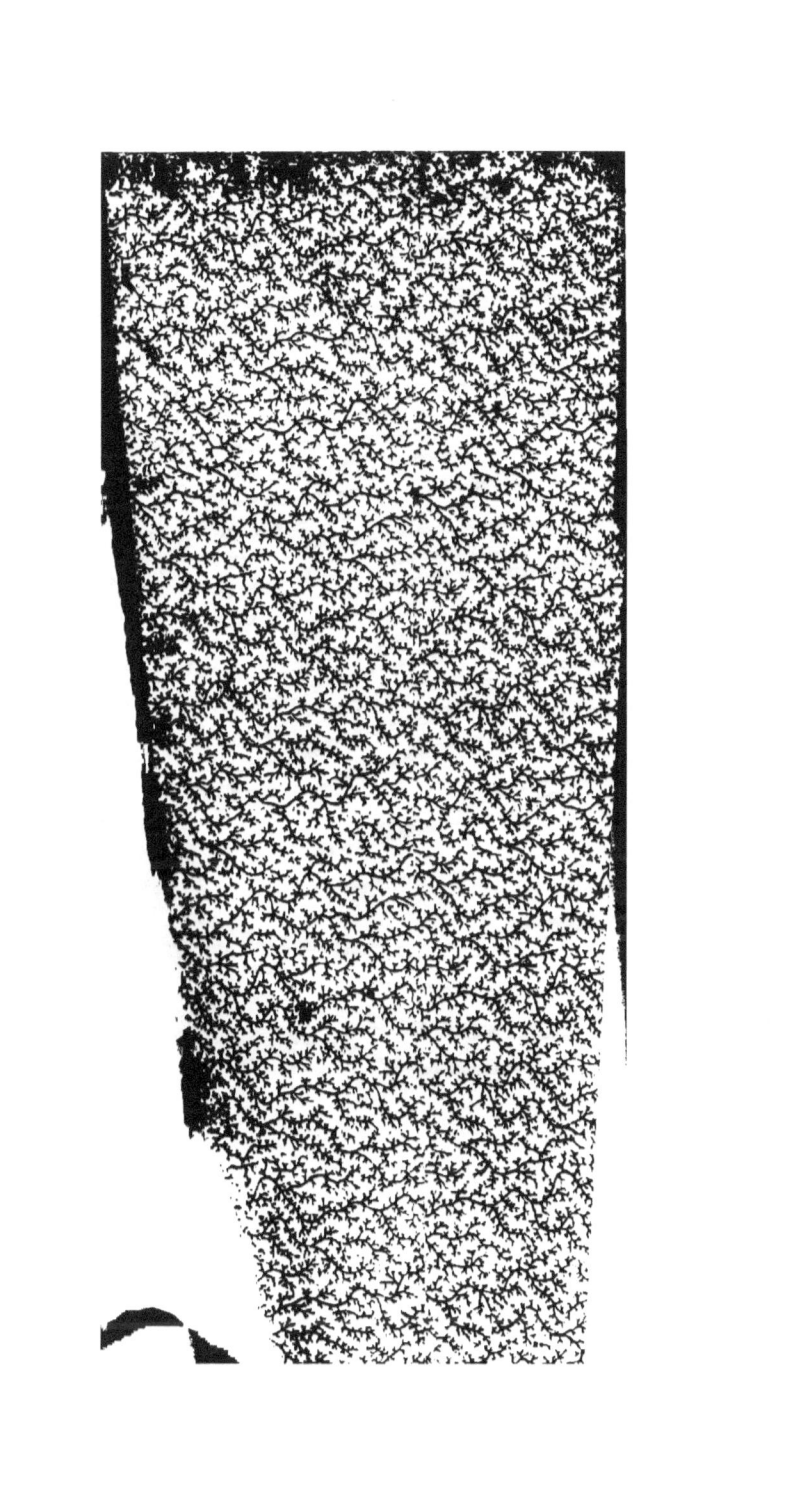

THE PEARLS

friar is a s
ociated with
In his ha
wise natur
of an enli
and gives hi
presents, as it
eaks, we seem t
himself as the p
monk, Shake
erience, and th
him. He wa
knew its weakn
hness; yet the
thy for his fello
eir weaknesses,
r duties; but, a
ping hand, and l
nger is he young
s error, and like
uly espouses the

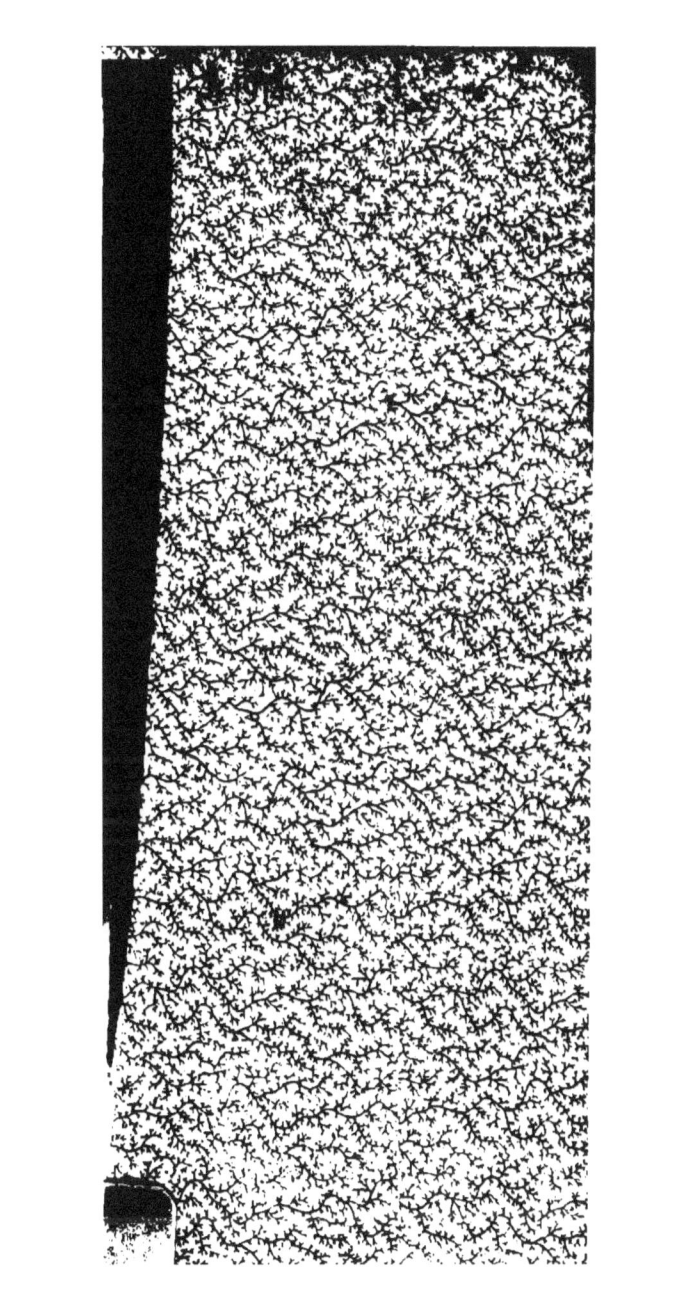

crowded into human existence. The balcony scene is the last gleam of this fleeting bliss. Heavenly accents float upon the air, the fragrance of the pomegranate blossoms is wafted aloft, the sighing complaint of the nightingale pierces the leafy shadows of the grove, and the trees can only in rustling and fragrance add their assent to that sublime, sad hymn upon the frailty of human happiness.

But where is the corpse of Romeo? What has become of Juliet? In a deserted street of deserted Verona stands, half-hidden, an old smoke-stained hostelry, where there is shouting, and swearing, and smoking, where macaroni and sour wine are dealt out to laborers. It was once the palace of the Capulets. Here Juliet lived. At the end of a court-yard there is an ancient tomb, the burial place, they tell you of Romeo and Juliet. It looks now like an empty ditch.

Every year more than a thousand curious people come on a pilgrim-age hither to see this fragment of stone. It is due to Shakespeare that the traveller now visits Verona solely to look for traces there of Romeo and Juliet.

Our Lady in Art.

WHEN the bright month of May comes to us, the wealth and beauty of spring sunshine and spring joy floods the earth telling of the rich harvests to be gathered during the months of summer. And this is the month the Church has dedicated to her who is full of grace and glory, because it is from her our Divine Redeemer took his mortal form. In the words of St. John: "God *became* man, and if He *became* man he had a mother," and she is justly entitled, therefore, to the chaplets of tender affection which the loyal children of the Church delight to weave for her. If we survey the works of art upon our

Lady we find, except in the case of one or two of the great masters, little to praise, before the end of the eighth century. The works before that time expressed religious thought, but left much to be desired in point of artistic execution. But during the ninth and tenth centuries a depth of feeling and a degree of artistic beauty in the representations of the Madonna were attained, which favorably compare with anything produced during the most flourishing periods of art in Italy. It is most natural to consider first those productions in which the Madonna is alone, or, as the Latins call her, the *Madonna Gloriosa*. In these we seldom find two representations of the same description, the subject being one which left the artist free to work out his own ideas without borrowing those of others. Well, too, have many succeeded, and we have a collection of works which for art, genius and religious feeling, cannot be surpassed. When the Madonna is seen alone holding a book in her hand she is known as *Virgo Sapientissima* and is then the patroness of those who search after wisdom. If she holds a sceptre or wears a crown she is called " *Regina Coeli.*" If a throng of angels are paying their tributes of honor to her she is the " *Regina Angelorum.*" If there is no distinguishing feature in the painting, but the Madonna is entirely alone, she is " Sancta Maria Virgo."

THE CORONATION OF THE VIRGIN. This subject was not a favorite one with sculptors for the simple reason that it was too difficult for manipulation in clay. The painters, however, frequently made this the subject of their efforts, and the result is that we have a bewildering variety of coronations. The features of those of early Christian art are totally distinct from later productions. In the former it is only Christ who crowns His Virgin Mother. They are both, as a rule, seated on the same throne, and not unfrequently we see the Eternal Father above. In the later representations we find that the deep feelings of the early artists are entirely disregarded and instead of religious grandeur a beautiful and picturesque scene is presented to us, either of the Madonna kneeling and receiving her crown at the hands of her Divine Son or of her crowning by the angels. In some pictures she is seated between the Father and the Son, who hold the crown about to be placed on her head, while in others the background presents a view of paradise with groups of rejoicing angels in the distance. One of the most beautiful coronations is that of Fra Angelico. The tender and pious spirit of that devout artist gleams in every line and every figure. A vesture of brilliant splendor robes the Redeemer who is seated on a throne of glory with His kingly crown upon His head. At His feet, a vision of graceful purity and humility, kneels His Virgin mother.

I think the Madonna's face is one of the most beautiful creations of Angelico. It wears a look of sublime meekness, of deep sorrow and yet overpowering joy, and of abiding love in Him who is to place upon her brow the crown of victory. Around the Madonna are choirs of angels robed in the brightest of celestial glory. It is wonderful in how short a time the eye appreciates and loves to see those bright colors, so constantly used by that wonderful artist. And the truth is that this use of rich colors by Angelico is only a characteristic indication of his greatness, for all artists possessed of truly noble sentiments love brilliant coloring. We frequently meet men who express themselves harshly on this feature of Angelico, but in so doing they only publish their own ideas and show their ignorance of the true purpose of art. For if we glance over the works of the famous artists we shall find that those who are coarse and sensual care little for delicate color, they only delight in gloomy brown and gray and gaudy red. There is nothing in them suggestive of that flashing, jewel-like coloring, so pure and chaste, the work of a man who has never harbored any thoughts save those that were noble and becoming a Christian. Now Angelico commands the loveliest colors within the vision of man, and this painting we are speaking of has the blue of the sky, the gold of the sunshine and the fairy clouds of filmy fleece in a perfection that is hardly credible. The lower part of the picture shows us the patriarchs, martyrs, apostles and saints who welcome our Lady to the reward so richly won. It is, in every way, a marvellous production and had Angelico left us no other painting than this, it alone would have been sufficient to place him among the greatest art geniuses of the world.

This work is treasured in the Church of St. Dominic, where Angelico was nurtured and made his profession as a monk. Of the other coronations of the Virgin it can only be said that they, in one respect, are all different in treatment and in another respect they do not differ. The Madonna for instance is always received with glory, and her robes are embroidered with the golden radiance of sun and moon. Many chapels are dedicated to Our Lady of the Coronation, and in several of these there are some fine examples on the subject to which the chapel is dedicated.

THE IMMACULATE CONCEPTION. The Immaculate Conception was a subject particularly favorable to the Spanish and Italian schools. The model of the Virgin in those representations is the Woman of the Apocalypse in all the beauty of Juda's fairest daughter—a spotless maid of twelve or fourteen years. She is invariably clothed in white with a blue mantle and her hands folded as if in prayer. It is in the Immaculate Conception that we see the sun, like a vivid light, around the hallowed person of the Virgin. The moon is beneath her feet and a crown of stars above her head. Murillo, the great Spanish painter, treated this subject many times and he is credited with having produced the profoundest as well as the most picturesque Conception of any artist. But there lived a painter not long before his time, known by the name of Roslas, who is justly praised for his Conceptions. Some, indeed, assert that he gave that gentle sentiment to his works which was usually given by the greatest Italian masters. Velasquez reached a high degree of perfection in his Conceptions. Their chief merit is the broad treatment shown throughout in every detail. The Virgin is here with her hands clasped and looking down as if at the people assembled before her. She is arrayed in a bright robe of pale violet color, while a dark blue mantle falls in graceful folds across her shoulders. The depth and solemnity of expression in these Madonnas are very striking, and the girlish features are well blended into a face of surpassing loveliness. The whole figure is generally relieved by fleecy clouds, the sun bursting brightly through them and above the head of the Virgin gleam the twelve stars. The Virgin generally stands on a half moon and, as is the case in one of his works, the moon is only partly illumined. Velasquez in his idea of the Conception is powerful and realistic and in none of his abstract works did he ever achieve so much fame and honor. Murillo, who painted his Conceptions so charmingly, always presents to us in his various works on this subject a great variety. Some have only two or three figures besides Our Lady, while others have more than thirty ; but through all of them there prevails the same deep thought and lively imagination. His most celebrated Conception, the one we are so accustomed to see about us in fine photographs and engravings, when the Madonna is standing on a crescent in the midst of clouds and choirs of cherubic faces, hardly needs a review here, for it is known in almost every household.

VIRGO GLORIOSA. The earliest of all the representations of the Blessed Virgin are those known as the *Virgo Gloriosa.* Of this we have many examples in our churches. The most celebrated Virgo Gloriosa is by Van Eyck. The Madonna is seated on a magnificent throne, her head encircled by a richly-jewelled crown and her features full of grace and stateliness. In one hand she holds a book opened on whose pages her eyes are bent. This symbol of the book is apt to give the Virgin the attributes of the queen of wisdom. But the figure of the Madonna is worthy of a lengthy description—so faithful and tender a portrait is it of all that is good and lovely in woman.

OUR LADY OF HELP.—By this title we mean those paintings of the Madonna which represent her intercessory power. We have of this class, paintings without number, many of singular beauty and all of deep devotion, for they portray that power which the mother has with the son, and which is removed in nature from that of the highest archangel or the most exalted saint. Sometimes Our Lady of Help stands with oustretched arms, the crown on her head and the veil covering her face where folds of her robe are supported by surrounding angels. Beneath this are those in quest of favors, the rich and the poor, the happy and the miserable. Sometimes the infant Saviour is with her to show the close union existing between them in their offices of goodness to men. For as her sinless perfection was for the sake of Emmanuel so from him she derives her power as Refuge of the Afflicted.

One of the most singular representations on this subject is the *Misericordia* by *Pietra della Francesca*, painted for the Hospital of Bargo, San Sepolcro, in the Apennines. Here the arms of the Virgin are outspread, her robe hanging in heavy folds, beneath which are gathered, kneeling, the sufferers who seek her aid. The celebrated *Misericodia di Lucca*, considered the greatest work of Fra Bartolomeo, was painted about the year 1515, a short time before the death of its painter. The portrayal of the Virgin here is particularly striking. In all her grandeur and beauty she stands on a raised platform, her arms extended and her head raised towards heaven; the drapery is upheld by angels. On one side of the picture is the donor who is represented by St. Dominic and just beneath the Virgin are grouped the various personages of Lucca asking her to obtain the cessation of the plague which in 1512 desolated a great part of nothern Italy. Above the Virgin, surrounded by a glory, is Christ with a host of angels. Taking this work as a whole it is very expressive, and, as Wilkie says, "the expression of the heads, the dignified beneficence of the Blessed Virgin, the dramatic feeling of the groups, particularly those of the women and children, justify its fame as one of the greatest productions of the human mind." In pictures of the Day of Judgment, Our Lady is always intended to be represented as the dispenser of mercy. She sits on the right hand of the Saviour and appears as a mediatress and interceding for mercy. In the well-known painting of the Last Judgment by Rubens, executed for the Jesuit Fathers of Brussels, the Virgin extends her robe over the world beneath as if to shield man from the wrath of her son.

THE VIRGIN AND CHILD.—The paintings of this class are so numerous and so full of tenderness and devotion that they merit a special article by themselves, and we must waive the consideration of them at present. It was under a picture of this description in a German village church that Coleridge saw the following cradle hymn which he rendered so beautifully in English.

> Dormi, Jesu ! mater ridet
> Quae tam dulcem somnum videt,
>   Dormi, Jesu ! blandule ;
> Si non dormis, mater plorat,
> Inter fila cantans orat,
>   Blande, veni, somnule.

> Sleep; sweet babe, my cares beguiling ;
> Mother sits beside thee smiling ;
>   Sleep, my darling, tenderly.
> If thou sleep not, mother mourneth,
> Singing as her wheels she turneth ;
>   Come, soft slumber, balmily.

The Story of Rebecca.

It was the time of pruning, when the south
Wind gently stirs the silver poplar leaf.
When the sheep and goat are on the hill, and hart
And roe so lightly skip 'mid groves of fig;
When flowers yield sweetest smell, and when the dove
In clift of rock and hollow of the wall
Is wont to coo his cadenced song of love.

When Abraham was worn and weak in age,
One day he Eleazar called, his first
And favored slave, and calmly said to him:
"Go thou to my own land and bring a wife
For Isaac—yea, it is the will of God,
He shall not marry 'mong the Chanaanites—"
And Eleazar swore he would obey.

When crests of Western hills were darkly seen,
And tiny dew drops lingered on the rose,
He took ten camels of his master's herd,
And chose the fairest one for Isaac's bride,
A stately brute of great brown sober eyes,
With glittering harness and with saddle-silk,
Bedecked with 'broidered coils and golden fringe.

And on they went across the rugged road
To Bathuel's home, in distant Syria's land,
And Nachor's city; and when even' came
They rested nigh a spring, where women drew
Its waters sweet, and there the servant prayed:
"O God, what one shall give a drink to me,
Let her be whom thou wills't for Isaac's choice."

And when he ends, behold, a comely maid,
With feet unsandalled and in simple robe,
Her loosened tresses playing with the wind
Stood there, and had her earthen pitcher filled,
She turned away, but when the servant spoke,
" Give me some water of the urn "—she let
The vessel quickly down upon her arm,

Then took her veil, and answered blushingly :
" Drink, drink, my lord, and let thy camels drink,
I trow thy journey has been very long
And wearied must thy faithful bearers be."
She poured the cool stone pitcher in the troughs ;
She smoothed the chosen camel with her hand,
And loosed the bonds that held the galling pack.

A casket Eleazar drew and gave to her,
Bright ear-rings made of gold and beads of pearl,
And coil'd bracelets of ten sickles weight,
" Thy name ? whose child art thou ? " She answered quick :
" Rebecca, I, the child of Bathuel : "
The maiden ran and told her mother all,
The slave of Abraham to Heaven prayed.

Rebecca had a brother, Laban named,
Who unto Eleazar went and said :
" Come in, thou blessed of God ; why stand'st thou here ?
I will prepare for thee and for thy train,
And feed and take thy camel's harness off."
His master's message Eleazar told :
Her loving father, Bathuel, was pleased.

'Twas night.   The camel ceased to munch the leaf.
And laid along the sand his wearied head,
The jackal's cry was heard along the plain,   .

The crane stood pensive near the reedy pool,
The pelican had stored his spacious pouch,
Nor raven's cry was heard. The sparrows call,
The cytisus had ope'd its bud. 'Twas morn.

And o'er the dusty way Rebecca rode,
The virgin bride upon her camel white
Unmindful of the scenes, so thoughtful she,
Of him who was to be her future spouse,
" I'll gird his sword for him and place the lance,
His bridal shall I hold when off he rides."
Thus did she think upon her future lord.

"And who is he who cometh toward the field ? "
She hailed at Agar's well, near Bersabee,
The husband of the voice of God—her fair
Form wrapped in Indian drapery and veil,
Seemed as a vision seen thro' Heaven's gate.
She heard his music voice—She saw his face
Dark eyes, she knew him true, who won her hand.

A Christmas Story.

IT WAS night; the full moonlight shone on the meadow uplands of
Judea, and the hilly country over by Bethlehem stood out in the
white glow. Every hill, and dell and copse seemed endowed with
greater and surpassing charms in the deceptive hues and illusive per-
spective of the moonlit night. Even the dusty road seemed a thing of
life, winding along like a streamlet between the darker fields and around
the hill to the village. The old square houses were silent and the village streets deserted. On the roof of the crowded khan could be seen

the sleeping forms of the guests. And they slept in peace, for the air was still. Not a breath of wind sighed through the valley; not a whisper was heard from the wood. The leaves of the olive hung motionless, and the palm trees drooped in silent sleep. The still heavens shone with inspiring beauty, unobscured by cloud or mist. The silence was broken only by the gurgling of the speeding brook, or, now and then, by a sleepy piping from the shepherd's flute.

Soon a sudden change was felt. A wind gust from the north hissed over the hilltop. It grew chilly and the grass quivered in the still night. Another gust, and another, and a light, cold breeze whispered through the wood. The breeze grew stronger and the sheep nestled closer together. The sleepers on the khan drew their blankets impatiently about them; a light dust eddied along the road. Still stronger the breeze grew; the olive quivered in the unusual chill and the sleepy palm woke with a start. All the slumbering echoes of nature were aroused, and the wind murmered through the village streets. Now, as the north wind sped down the valley, floating on the chilly air, high above the shivering of the awakened trees was heard a slow northern ballad:

SONG OF THE NORTH WIND.

From the Baltic snows,
  To Siberia's sand
Where the Obi flows,
  Thor the mighty,
  Thor the thunderer,
Thor was the god of the land.

Thor was cruel and bad,
Northern lands were sad,
  And hated they his beard
That makes the lightning flash;
And at the thunder's crash,
  They thought of Thor and feared.

And the years slipped by,
    Till thro' heaven bright
Heard I the hopeful cry,
        Christ the Lord,
        Christ the Saviour,
    Christ is come this night.

From the Arctic north
Come I joyous forth,
    To see the Christ on earth,
South, from the frozen seas,
Borne on the chilly breeze,
    To be present at His birth.

The song ceased and the echoes died away in the woodlands. The wind has lost its driving force and it is still. One can almost see the air, so cold it is, so settled is the frost. The dust has hardened on the road. But lo! borne down the valley on the breeze and glistening on the night is the form of a giant warrior of the north. He is encased in a chain-like armor of ice and sings to the bright sky: '

            I am the wind;
            Out from the Arctic north
        Where ice doth bind
            The sea, have I come forth.

He rests on the hilltop and his heroic figure is outlined against the sky. Glistening icicles hang from his red beard, and his head is hoary with the snow of untold winters. The rugged, northern features are rough and browned from the cutting wind; the hoar frost clings to him and glistens in the moonlight; his eyes gleam brighter than the frost. And now, as the moon rises higher, each sparkling little frost drop is seen to be a tiny angel. Every dark blade of grass on the hillside shines with diamond lustre. They have peopled all the mea- dows, these bright heavenly beings, and their soft whisperings rise on the icy night like sweet music.

As the grim old Northern seats him on the hillside there is a soft murmur from the eastward, and an angel zephyr of warm wind smoothes his snow-bound temples. The murmur from the east grows deeper, and from afar sounds the melody of sweet singing. All the echoes of heaven and earth seem to unite in exquisite harmony. And now, as the breeze strengthens and the east wind draws near, he can catch the words of the song.

SONG OF THE EAST WIND.

O'er a glowing eastern valley,
    On the liquid air I float
    In a priceless pearly boat,
In a zephyr-wafted galley;
    Thro' my airy realm of dreams
    Coursing on its limpid streams.

Gliding through the silent heaven
    With its glowing orbs of light,
    On the magic air of night,
By the murmuring zephyrs driven;
    Floated I in purest gladness,
    Never touched by aught like sadness.

In the eastern heavens glowing,
    In the Persian land afar
    There appeared a wondrous star
Bringing fear to the unknowing;
    But I joyed; it told the birth
    Of the Christ upon this earth.

All the air with song is ringing
    With a harmony profound,
    With a soft melodious sound
Of the angels sweetly singing.
    O'er the heavenly lake I skim
    To the hills of Bethlehem.

As the song ceased the east wind could be seen riding on the night. She was seated in a wide shell pinnace. The mast was ivory and the sails were pearly cloth. The pinnace was formed entirely of pearls, and when it glided out into the white moonlight, it glowed with unspeakable beauty. She herself was a dark-haired eastern maid. Her complexion was richer than the olive, and her dreamy eyes dwelt in expressive wonder on the the icy north wind. She was clothed in flowing robes of cashmere, studded with white diamonds. Her attendants glowed with all the wealth of the east. The emerald zephyrs leapt from the pearly pinnace and were lost in the green meadow. But a soft musical murmur rose from the ground as they sped away with the frost angels among the grasses.

She alighted on the hilltop, and the rugged old wind rose with a courtly grace and said, " Dark-haired daughter of the east welcome." She sang in reply, and the song was music to him. It seemed a heavenly melody in his rude, northern ears. He listened in delicious rapture:—

> Tell me, O my northern father,
> O thou glittering, frosty king,
> Hast thou heard the gladd'ning tidings
> Thro' thy icy regions ring?

And he answered:

> Far in the northern sky
> The Christ, the angels sing;
> I heard the joyous cry
> And come to greet the King.

And then he said, " Thy brother, the wild southern, is he coming?" And even as he spoke a bright, starry cross, passing description, shone out in the southern sky. "My brother? He is come, O father!" she said, pointing to the south. And far in the distance was heard a low rumble as of wheels, and the hissing of a lash. The wind soon appeared in sight, dashing furiously through the heavens high above the village.

The southern cross blazed from his forehead.   He stood erect in a low golden chariot drawn by winged steeds.   The horses were black as ebony and the fire of the desert glowed from their nostrils.   The wind himself was a young Colossus, perfect in form and feature.   His eyes shone bright as stars, and his black locks were covered with sand from his wild pranks in the desert.   Now he threw the jeweled lash he flourished into the chariot, and sang:

SONG OF THE SOUTH WIND.

I love the fairy southern land ;
I sport me in the wild oasis,
The star of all the desert sand,
   The gem that all the desert graces.

When high the dreamy moon was soaring,
I heard the truant winds adoring
   The Saviour of this night ;
From out the spring the strain rose higher,
The sands sang like an angel choir
   The coming of the Light.

He neared the hill, and reining in his foaming steeds, turned toward the East wind, and said in low, musical tones:

"O, sister! yesternight the sands sang the Christ; the spirit of life was in them, but to-day! they are parched and dry; the fair oasis is dried up in the baking air; my steeds are impatient; they paw the ground in their thirst; all the south languishes for the cooling breezes from the eastward; my sister has forgotten them."

"Nay," she answered slowly, "I sent the cooling zephyrs and they perished in the sand-storm."

"True," he said; "I sent my courier wind to summon you; the wind was parched and tore up the ground in its impatience, and whirled the sand on high.   And have the cooling zephys perished?"   She shook her head, sadly; and he tore his hair with grief.   "I'll chide the sand and the blast," he said; "they have vexed my eastern sister. But the desert! the south! the south is perishing!"

And even as he spoke, a murmur came from the south as of sweet singing. "Ah," he said, "the zephyrs are not dead; they have refreshed the drooping south; the south is singing the Christ."

While these two had been conversing the North wind was sitting sadly on the hillside, facing the west. "Ah," he said aloud, when the Southern had spoken, "I fear my fair-haired daughter of the West is not coming." They all three looked eagerly westward. And immediately a big spray of ocean drops fell on the group; and turning they saw the laughing West wind standing on the hilltop. She was a small brown-haired maiden. A bright star shone in her bosom. Her eyes were laughing and mischievous, and her cheeks glowed redder than the setting sun. The glittering spray clung to her robes and shone like gems in the moonlight. In her hand she carried a bow, the ends tipped with copper, and a quiver slung behind her was full of silver-tipped arrows.

"Star of the West!" said the south wind, in his low musical tones, "didst thou see the desert in thy flight?"

"I have but come thence," was the answer. "I stole upon you from the southward, while you were intent on the west. When I was speeding over the ocean I heard the low moan of the desert. I could not bear that any should be sad at such a happy time. I turned from my course. I refreshed the fainting south, and cooled the parched sands; and now in their joy they are singing the Christ."

"Daughter of the West," said the North wind, "when did you hear the glad news of the Christ's coming?" And she sang in answer:

SONG OF THE WEST WIND.

'Twas in the dreamy twilight hours,
When daylight, trembling, fearful cowers
Before the night, and saddens every gloaming,

That loud I heard the joyful cries,
From deep-enraptured nature rise ;
That sang the Christ, that sang the Saviour's coming.
From every land and sea,
Uprose the song of praise to me,
In one grand burst of rapturous melody.
I longed to see the Christ this night,
And eastward fled in speeding flight,
In flight far swifter than the lightning, driven ;
High o'er the troubled, fearful seas,
Borne in the arms of my loved breeze,
In one entrancing flight thro' ringing heaven
And I was happy, whiles
I heard below for lengthening miles,
A chant of gladness from the sea-girt isles.

Scarce had the echoes of the song died away, than loud rang a cry through the heavens. The hosanna of the angels re-echoed through the valley; the very air sang in joy. The trees waved their branches as if in triumph. On the roof of the Khan the sleepers woke in alarm, and listened, trembling. The shepherds started in affright; the sheep fled through the pasture. The bleak North wind sped down to the cavern where the Christ was born. He was lying in His mother's arms; and her sweet, maternal face dwelt on the infant before her with a yearning, unspeakable love. Back further in the cavern, Joseph was fixing a sputtering torch in the rocky walls. Beside him an old ox gazed vacantly into space with his mild eyes, and continually shifted from side to side.

" I adore Thee
O my King ! "

was all the Northern said. The child smiled on the grand, heroic figure; but shivered in the cold, and nestled closer to His Mother. And

so the wind sped to the hilltop.   He turned toward the East wind,
" Go thou down, my dark-haired daughter and adore the Christ."

The pinnace glided down on the warmer air and the wind sang at
the grotto:

> "Child of Light ! Child-God from Heaven,
> Join I in the angels' pæan ;
> Meek I bow in adoration,
> At my hidden God's oblation."

The emerald zephyrs caressed the Child's soft features, and the pinnace glided toward the awakening East.   The South wind drove down
to the cavern.   The black steeds neighed joyously, and the wind sang
sweetly:

> "I love Thee ! O, Thou King of Kings,
> And in my love have taken wings,
> And sped from southern lands and sea,
> To swear, oh ! King, my fealty."

But the Child slept in the cheering warmth from the south; and the
wind drove desertward at a furious pace.   And last the whispering
West wind greeted the new-born King :

> " Far from the land of the West,
> Over the sounding sea,
> Come I, O God of heaven,
> Come I to honor Thee."

Suddenly in one grand burst of song, countless thousands of angels
appeared in the opened heavens, and sang the eternal anthem of peace.
The wind hurried back to the hilltop.   But down the white road approached a wondering, fearing band of shepherds; and the winds shrank
from mortal gaze.   The bright-eyed Western maiden floated away over
the dark meadows, and the grim Northern fled from the open hill.   As
he swept through the echoing valley, he turned for one last look at the

scene.   In the bright heavens above the myriad angels sang in unison ;
below, the shepherds knelt before the crib in silent adoration..   And as
he sped further to the north, ever faintly and more faintly, the sweet
refrain of the angel's song was borne to him on the sounding air:

> " Glory to God in the heavens,
> Peace to men of good will."

Which is King?

ONE evening, as I lay tired and weary over my class books, I heard
a number of voices speaking in the utmost confusion.   After the
din had somewhat subsided, I found that there was a debate among the
speakers as to who should be king.   What was my surprise when I saw
that the voices came from the books I had been studying, namely, my
Geography, English Grammar, Phaedrus' Fables and Catechism.   By
mutual consent the books, in order of size, were to give their opinions
as to who should be king.

The Geography, therefore, being the largest, began first: " My
causes for superiority," he said, " are many, but I shall be brief.   If it
were not for me, this great country would never have been discovered;
but for me you seldom could travel, and then but a short distance;
through me, you know, you live in this vast country; I have aided in
adding to the long list of martyrs; I also have helped in winning numberless souls to God.   Why, then, do you object to me as king?   Will
any of you tell me of a more useful life ?   If so, I shall yield willingly
to his command."

Then the English Grammar, stretching himself out to his full English,
began: " What my large companion has related I acknowledge is all
quite true, but how could geography be written were it not for

orthography, one of my four principal parts? How could the great preachers and missionaries learn the different languages in which they preached, and thus win souls in countless numbers to heaven, were i not for me? In all *modesty*, I ask, how, but for me, could the most powerful nations of the earth speak, read and write correctly? I believe it a settled question, unless my companions tell a better tale, that I shall be your king."

Having thus told his story, the books were waiting patiently for the Catechism, which was next in size, to begin. Seeing that he was in deep thought they motioned to the Fables to proceed. This book, despite its small size, rose on its extensive margin and cast a disdainful look around. "As far as your reasons go," said he, pertly addressing the Geography and Grammar, "I am certain of being the leader, for your reasons are perfectly useless. I, however, give sound advice to all. I amuse some, others see in me a great many things well worth imitating. I teach all of you not to be proud, not to despise what it is little, for oftentimes that which is little proves of great use. In fact, my wisdom is so great that you would probably be tired should I manifest it to you. So now, without more ado, let us listen to our silent friend, the Catechism, and our doom shall be sealed."

The Catechism now began: "I have heard all of your reasons," he said, "and, certainly, some of them are very good. The Geography would be of no use without the Grammar, the Grammar without the Geography, and the Phaedrus without the Grammar. I, however; teach you of your God, who made the languages, missionaries, souls, worlds and all things. Let us all unite together, keep in our own place, be content with our lot and try to benefit our neighbors. Then shall we be, indeed, happy."

The other books immediately raised a cry, and called out for the Catechism to be their king. "Not so," it answered; "let us, as I have said, live together in peace and contentment, for those only can rule well who have well learned to obey." I awoke and saw the Catechism on the top of the other books, and all waiting patiently to be used in turn for the morrow's lesson.

The Tale of a Falling Star.

Fair was the night in the June time of flowers;
   The moon full and placid was half through her round
The drip of the fountains beneath the green bowers
   Kept tune to the zither's melodious sound.
The glittering jewels that spangled the sky
Kept a sentinel watch from their towers on high.

The breeze from the Occident softly was sighing;
   The nightingale sang the sad tale of her woes;
Bright pearlets of dew were contentedly lying
   On the petals of hyacinth, tulip and rose:
Upon the green sward, like the heavens at night,
The glow-worms, like stars, gave a luminous light.

Breathing the perfume that rose from the garden;
   The cool air of evening; the scent from the bowers;
Of nature's great treasures the one silent warden,
   I sat at my window and counted the hours.
'Mong the slow dripping fountains; beneath the pale moon:
'Mid the soft Persian vales; in the mild month of June.

Long did I watch while the glittering cluster
   Of planets unnumbered swept on through the gloom.
Like the lamps of the faithful whose flickering lustre
   Shines high o'er the altars of Mecca and Koom,
But lo, with a flash that bewilders the eye,
A meteor falls from its throne in the sky.

THE PEARLS OF A YEAR.

Scarce had it fallen when sweet from afar
  On the soft evening zephyr the melody swells
Of a baritone voice to a tinkling guitar,
  Whose varying strokes sound like faint fairy bells.
Louder the voice grew and sweeter and strong,
And through the still night rose the low plaintive song:

      " O star that fallest from on high
        Into an endless depth below,
      Why leavest thou a peaceful sky
        To seek a world of woe?

      Swifter than the wild career
        Of shivering lightning was thy motion:
      Ah! whither dost thou disappear
        Behind the southern ocean?

      Endless, endless is thy flight
        Through unknown tracts of airy waste:
      Through regions of eternal night
        Forever must thou haste!

      No more, no more we'll see thee shine,
        When slowly fades the golden day:
      No more the dome of Mecca's shrine
        Shall mirror back thy ray!

      O fiery brand of angels' ire
        Hurled at some darksome fiend of night,
      Who dared invade the heavenly choir
        To catch one glimpse of light.

      O hapless spirit falling fast
        From the bright regions of the blest,
      Thy dream of happiness is past;
        No more thy soul shall rest!

O, thou that wert a lesser gem
  'Mong those that everlasting shine
In nature's God's bright diadem
  An humbler lot is thine!

Swift star farewell! In future, when
  I wander by the endless shore,
Thy quiet beam I'll see again
  Far brighter than before!"

Then ceased the song and calm Silence returning
  With robes faintly rustling swept quick through the vale.
The glow-worms had long ceased their translucent burning:
  The rose drooped in grief at the nightingale's tale.
But scarce had the notes of the song died away
When from the pale East gleamed the first rays of day.

The Charms of Fiction.

NOTHING more unfairly represents what a man thinks than a newspaper report of what he was supposed to say ; but there are some plain statements which may be accepted as true even if they do appear as reports.   Thus when a lecturer is recently reported to have said that novel reading is pernicious, and that Scott, Dickens, Bulwer, and many more have introduced a dangerous delight into literature, there is something so credible and simple in the statement that there is little reason to suppose the lecturer did not say it.

It is certainly a curious proposition, and yet it is one frequently made. It is curious because the literature of fiction is only the permanent flower of the imagination. It is in letters what painting and sculpture, architecture and music, are, in forms and colors and sounds. It is as instinctive and inevitable as smiling and weeping, as all emotion whatsoever. To represent truth allegorically—to delineate the operation of principle and passion—to signalize the moral of human action and human life—to show the essential and triumphant loveliness of virtue—to preserve in enduring lines the most humorous and eccentric, the most nefarious and base, the most noble and inspiring characteristics of men and times—all these are the substance of the novel and the work of the novelist.

And it is in a work of observation and of imagination as it is in effective preaching. The author or the preacher must first have eyes to see, then fancy to feel, and at last electric expression to strike home the gathered results. But in its essence, story-telling is the earliest desire and the simplest instinct. The wild rhymes that soothe the child— the impossible Mother Hubbards and Houses that Jack built, and blissful melodious nonsense of Mother Goose, which are as universal as baby-hood—what are they but appeals and inspirations to that vague, vast power of the imagination which colors life and death, and in its act of highest creation is reverentially called genius, as most aptly sympathizing with the great divine energy of creation.

The love of music, of color, of form—the delight in natural beauty, in the perfume of flowers, and the purple outline of distant mountains, and in a higher degree the fascination of noble, heroic and saintly character, all these are strictly related to the imagination, and its play and pleasure is the reproduction of them.

But when the critic questions the morality of novels, is he not treading dangerous ground? What is a novel? It is a picture of life. Just in the degree that it is a true novel, it is an accurate representation— within such limits of space and time and mutual relation as to make it effective and real in its impression and influence—of the characters and circumstances which surround us all and with which we are most familiar.   It is, in one word, what Shakspeare calls the drama " holding the mirror up to nature."

Then what is the object of a novel?   As it is a work of art, its object is gratification of the sense of fitness and symmetry ; in other words intellectual delight.   But then, as it is a panorama of human action, its necessary result is human improvement.   For every man recognizing in himself the elements of character delineated, recognizes also the fidelity of the picture of their inevitable operation in life—sees himself openly revealed—his secret sympathies, impulses, ambitions—his vices, his virtues, his temptations ; and follows with terrible fascination the course of his undeveloped future, pauses thoughtful and alarmed, and hangs back upon the very edge of sorrow and destruction.

This is the inevitable moral of a novel as it is of life.   The novelist himself writes to picture the play of character, but in doing that he does the other.   An architect builds a beautiful house for a man to live in, but in building it he also quickens the sense of beauty in every beholder.   A painter reproduces upon canvas the form and features of a beautiful woman, but in doing it he also restores in all its splendor her life and character to those who know her.

Of course it is not to be supposed that men always write stories with this distinct intention.   Sir Walter Scott himself declared that a novelist could only hope to amuse—a remark which shows plainly enough that Sir Walter could do his work much better than he could talk about it.

"We are inclined," says he, " to think that the worst evil to be apprehended from the perusal of novels is that the habit is apt to generate an indisposition to real history and useful literature, and that the best that can be hoped is that they may sometimes instruct the youthful mind by real pictures of life, and sometimes awaken their better feelings and sympathies by strains of generous sentiments and tales of fictitious woe. Beyond this point they are a mere elegance, a luxury contrived for the amusement of polished life, and the gratification of that half love of

literature which pervades all ranks in an advanced state of society, and
are read much more for amusement than with the least hope of deriving
instruction from them."

Do you suppose that Scott sincerely believed mankind were to be
more improved by reading the real history of Messalina, of Cleopatra,
of Aspasia, and Catharine, than by the fictitious story of Jean Deans?
Did he really suppose the long histories of idiotic emperors in moribund
Rome and Asia to be "useful literature," and "The Vicar of Wake-
field" to be "a mere elegance, a luxury contrived for the amusement
of polished life? Did he prefer, as a moralist and a lover of his kind,
that his daughters should read the true memoirs of the Duke of Gram-
mont or Charles II., or of almost any other king, rather than the untrue
memoirs of Sir Roger de Coverley? Did Sir Walter Scott write novels
so long and so well with such a feeling as this, and without knowing
that the excellence of a novel is the excellence of nature, and of every
other great work of art, and that his own Rebecca is as real in herself,
and as influential in her degree upon the human mind, as Judith and
Queen Elizabeth?

All history slowly becomes romance. Is Alaric, the Visigoth, as real
a person, in any serious sense, as Mr. Pickwick or Mr. Dombey? It is
much more important to have a religious and manly tone of life incul-
cated in any way than it is to know that the Egyptian Ammunoph the
4th succeeded Ammunoph the 3d. Suppose there was such a man as
Oliver Cromwell, who is admitted into history without question. Now
his interest for me is the influence his story has upon my life; and yet
how am I to know what kind of a man he was? I open the books, and
I get an enemy's sneer or a friend's flattery. In the first book he is the
first of heroes—in the next, he is the last of hypocrites. Probably
history is less true to nature, upon the whole, than Fiction. Clio is
such a high-stepping muse that she goes over just what we want to
know. Hence memoirs over which presides our haughty muse, but

the delightful Goddess of Gossip are the best history, and good memoirs are, like good novels, true pictures of life.

There is no need of comparisons, but there is no doubt that the history of Robinson Crusoe would help a boy in his way through life as much as any history of Oliver Cromwell.

Great qualities, heroism, energy sweetness, character, prudence, foresight—these are what the mind craves, and it knows and values them wherever they are, and gets its moral out of them in quite the same way, whether the story be of the real Alexander or the imaginary Achilles. Goodness is never imaginary. History and fiction are only two ways of putting a fact. We are just as sorry to see Iago succeed as to see Leonidas fail. For us both Iago and Leonidas are actual men ; the form of the story neither affects them nor us. "Men will not become highwaymen," says Dr. Johnson, "because Macbeth is acquitted on the stage." And it is equally true that they will still pick pockets, though the historical Turpin swung at Tyburn.

Thackeray, in the Cornhill magazine, speaks very wisely concerning novels and novel-reading. In the quaint little town of Chur, far away among the Grisons, he used to encounter a lazy, slouching, half-grown boy, with big feet, and lazy hands dawdling out of scanty pantaloons and tight sleeves, poring over a little book so intently that he had no eye for the purple evening, the apple-woman, or the rosy apple-cheeked maidens prattling around the fountain—no thought for the morrow's lessons, of the good mother waiting supper, or the father preparing a sound scolding—utterly absorbed in that little book It was a novel, of course ; for nothing else could so have entranced the young reader. Whereupon the novelist editor thus moralizes :

" Have you ever seen a score of white-bearded, white-robed warriors, or grave seniors of the city, seated at the gate of Jaffa or Beyrout, and listening to the story-teller reciting his marvels out of ' Antse ' or the ' Arabian Nights ' ? I was once present, when a young gentlemen at table put a tart away from him, and said to his neighbor the younger son (with rather a fatuous air), 'I never eat sweets.'

"'Not eat sweets ; and do you know why ?' says T."

"'Because I am past that kind of thing,' says the young gentleman."

"'Because you are a glutton and a sot!' cries the elder (and Juvenis winces a little). 'All people who have natural, healthy appetites love sweets ; all children, all women, all Eastern people whose tastes are not corrupted by gluttony and strong drink.' And a plate full of raspberries and cream disappeared before the philosopher."

You take the allegory ? Novels are sweets. All people with healthy literary appetites love them—almost all women—a vast number of clever, hard-headed men. Why, one of the most learned professors in the city said to me, only yesterday, 'I have just read So-and-So for the second time' (meaning one of Lew Wallace's exquisite fictions) Judges, bishops, statesmen, students are notorious novel-readers ; as well as young boys and sweet girls and their kind, tender mothers. Who has not read about Eldon, and how he cried over novels every night when he was not at whist ?

As for that lazy, naughty boy at Chur, I doubt whether *he* will like novels when he is thirty years of age. He is taking too great a glut of them now. He is eating jelly until he will be sick. He will know most plots by the time he is twenty, so that *he* will never be surprised when the Stranger turns out to be the rightful earl—when the old waterman, throwing off his beggarly gabardine, shows his stars and the collars of his various orders, and clasping Antonia to his bossom prove himself to be the prince, her long lost father. He will recognize the novelists' same characters, though they appear in knightly armor, or the garb of the nineteenth century. He will get weary of sweets as boys of private schools grow tired of their pudding at dinner.

And pray what is the moral of this apologue? The moral I take to be this : the appetite for novels extending to the end of the world—far away in the frozen deep, the sailors reading them to one another during the endless night ; far away under the Syrian stars, the solemn sheiks and elders hearkening to the poet as he recites his tales ; far away in the camps, when the soldiers listen to some soothing story, after the hot day's march ; far away in little Chur yonder, where the lazy boy pores over the fond volume, and drinks it in with all his eyes ; the demand being what we know it is, the merchant must supply it, as he will supply tobacco and coffee to his wealthy patrons. But as surely as the young man smokes too much tobacco it will disagree with him ; and, so surely, dear reader, will too much novels cloy on thee.

How we Americans delight in recalling memories of that sweet symmetric life of Washington Irving, whom we all loved more than we ever loved any other man. Yet what was his work, what was it that made him at once so dear and so famous ?

It was not his histories, excellent as they are, any more than it was Scott's Life of Napoleon Bonapart, that gave him his crown of affection and admiration. No, it was the exquisite play of his fancy and his humor, and that kindly charity which always accompanies them. Irving is the author of the " Knickerbocker," of the " Sketch Book " and " Bracebridge Hall," of the " Alhambra," and the " Conquest of Granada." Soft, sunny lights lie on all he touched. Has he poisoned any fountain of pleasure or instruction ?

And if it should be replied, No, that he was always gentle and pure, but that others are prurient and seductive, the response is that the rule must not be construed from the exception.

And what account shall we make of the instinct which reaches out toward Irving so lovingly as toward all the story tellers or imaginative writers ? For in every forecastle and by every fireside, from Homer's Tale of Troy down to Robert Louis Stevenson's " Strange Case of Dr. Jekyll and Mr. Hyde," the story teller is always welcome.

What are the novelists but the story tellers in the long march and bivouac of life?

A few solitary scholars listen with respect to Aristotle ; a few grave men walk with Plato in the garden ; but when Sir Walter Scott begins the whole world becomes a boy again, and sits upon his knee delighted. Since Shakespeare, is there any fame so enviable and wide-spread as Scott's? To write a book which the boy reads in play time, and the mother in the nursery, and the statesman at midnight, and the general upon the eve of battle, and the girl puts with tears under her pillow, for an early start in the morning, this is to become a personal friend of the world.

The Old Mill.

A FEW years ago, while stopping in the country, I was wont to sit in the shade of an old mill on the bank of a little stream, and watch it flow by. It was my custom when tired to lie down in the soft grass ; and once when I was quietly dozing there I heard the great mill, at the request of its friend, the stream, tell the history of *his* life. "I was built," he said. "nearly seventy or eighty years ago, by more than sixty men. For fifty years I worked hard with your kind assistance, and thus helped my owner to support his family. But now I have grown old and no longer fit for use. However, if you will keep it a secret I will tell you what I now contain." The stream very willingly gave its consent, and I could almost hear the grass beside me moving to and fro, I kept so quiet. "As you know well," the mill continued, "for the past twenty years there has been a great deal of smuggling going on in this part of the country. The smugglers have chosen me as the place to hide their goods. If you could but profit by my stores I would be pleased to let you have them all, though I am afraid they would be of little value to you. On my top floor, in a little niche which you would scarcely perceive, is a ring which was lost by the smugglers. This caused the death of one of their number in a quarrel. It is my sad duty to guard his remains which lie in a wooden box safely hidden in the space between the floor and the ceiling of the room, and below another long and narrow chest. This chest is filled with gold to the amount of some ten thousand pounds. The chest is made of iron, and placed with its treasure in its present position by the man whose bones now rest above it. Thus in death he seems to guard the treasure which in life he collected with so much pains.

On my second floor are a number of bales of cotton, of tobacco and of an endless variety of things, while on the first floor is the room where the smugglers met. On this floor they divided the booty and held all their meetings." The stream during the story had apparently stopped. It was so very interesting that I held my own breath so as not to lose a word when, all of a sudden, I awoke. What about the dead body, and the gold, and the smugglers? thought I to myself. What if it were true ! Would not the gold be a fortune to me? But then it was guarded by a corpse and I began to fear that the ghost might attack me, and concluded not to disturb the dead.

I slowly wended my way home, musing all the time on my wonderful dream. The next day I walked in the direction of the mill, but imagine my surprise when I saw that during the night it had been burned to the ground. For many hours I searched the ruins, and at last came upon two boxes. Both were of the same size, but one was of iron. My eyes examined them carefully, and, as I thought, detected inside the iron chest, which had been partly burst by the heat some gold pieces. I immediately seized it, but as quickly let go my hold. With a few blows of a hammer I broke the box and eagerly looked at the contents.

There were twenty times the amount the mill had mentioned in his story. I was trying to carry it off when I was suddenly startled by a hand which placed itself on my shoulder, and b·· a great round something falling upon me. I struggled and turned and saw that it was the huge wheel of the mill pressing upon me. I gave a scream, for above it I saw the grinning skeleton of the murdered man, who, in a terrible voice, commanded me never to interfere with anything that did not belong to me. The wheel moving with a terrible rumbling, threated to crush me if I ever again profited by eavesdropping, even though I did not intend it. I promised to obey, and no sooner had I done so, and started away, than I awoke. Then I found myself, not in the field, nor in the mill, but safely stowed away in my own bed. I had dreamt, indeed, about the mill, about sleeping on the green grass, the finding of the gold, and the appearance of the ghosts. The next day when I saw the mill it was as still, gloomy and silent as ever, the stream seemed to laugh at me as it rippled by, and when I looked at the wheel which seemed to gaze like a huge unwinking eye, it appeared to make a solemn warning as if to say, Beware! Never listen to what your neighbors may have to say to each other.

The Song of the Ave Maria.

Ave Maria! Ave Maria!
The ocean chanteth along the strand,
Ave Maria! Ave Maria!
Re-echoes the music from out the land.

Far from the depths of unseen ocean,
Sounded that cry of grand devotion
         Sweetly to me;
Angels are singing it, soft it is winging it
         Over the sea.
Softer than sound of fountain,
      Sweeter than song of bird,
Over the cloud-loved mountain
      The heavenly music is heard.
From ocean to ocean, far and near,
Riseth the praise so wondrous clear,
      The convent bells and nature's dells
            Are sounding the Ave Maria.

         Ave Maria! Ave Maria!
Hark! to the song of the May,
         Ave Maria! Ave Maria!
Brightening all the day.
      Sweet is the night but far sweeter the dawning,
      When clear on the wings of the hastening morning
            Thy melody thrills
With lingering fleetness, and fills with its sweetness
            The echoing hills.
      The wakening May thus without us,
         Hence with the winter of sin!
      The spell of the May thus about us
         How can it be kept from within?
From ocean to ocean, far and near
Riseth the praise so wondrous clear,
      In our hearts we guard thee and sweet the refrain be
            As we sing the Ave Maria.

The Story of the First Pentecost.

ANALYSIS, as the word itself implies, consists in taking a work to pieces, stripping it of all ornament and examining its parts and elements. It is obvious to all that to make an analysis of an object is the only way to understand it thoroughly. For it is only when we thus take an object to pieces, examine part by part, the special qualities of each part and their relation to the whole, that we fully appreciate the power and intellect displayed in the whole.

If we wish to teach a person how to use a complicated machine, the first thing for us to do is to show him the structure complete, that he may take in at a glance its finished appearance and ultimate end. The next step would be to take the machine apart to show him the component pieces and their relative position. The third step would be to show how each part was made, and let the learner see them all in minute detail lying together.

This process of successive steps is analysis, a word derived from the Greek verb ἀναλύω, to separate into elements. It is the very best way to appreciate the speeches of great orators, for we are thus brought face to face with the skill shown by a master in the building up of a work of art. By this means also, we perceive the weakness of other speeches which we probably considered worthy of praise, but which, when put to the test of the dissecting knife of a severe analysis, when their weightiest arguments are reduced to syllogistic form, are shown to be weak and unworthy of our consideration.

Analysis is also very useful for the development of a critical mind and a literary taste; just as in the case of material objects, if we wish to test their strength or weakness we must weigh and test minutely the component parts.

If we carefully consider the works of good and bad writers we shall find the reason of the excellence of the former and the inferiority of the latter. The works of good authors, strong as may be the test applied to them, will always show their worth; while in bad writings, no matter how weak the test may be, the blemishes will show forth. This analysis of speeches forms one of the most pleasant tasks of students of rhetoric, and it is surprising how much knowledge one gains in following out the evolution of one leading thought.

One of the finest models of the gradual development of a leading thought is found in the speech of St. Peter, delivered on the day of Pentecost to an audience intensely opposed to him, sneering at his doctrines and ridiculing him and his fellow apostles. This speech is found in the 2d chapter of the Acts of the Apostles, and extends from the 14th to the 36th verse.

Shortly before a marvellous change had taken place in the apostles; the Holy Spirit had come down upon them, had inspired them with zeal, had inflamed their hearts with a desire of spreading Christ's doctrine, and they, burning with a divine enthusiasm, had gone forth boldly and fearlessly, declaring that Jesus whom the Jews had crucified was the Messiah. What caused still greater wonder, what had attracted far more attention and what was far more remarkable, the apostles spoke in different languages; the rude fishermen had become accomplished linguists and were equal to the task of preaching the gospel of Christ to all nations.

Their fame spread throughout the land, Jerusalem was in a turmoil, the enemies of Christ refused to credit the sincerity of what was taking place; every slur was cast upon the apostles, their enemies raised a storm of abuse against them, and some even charged their unusual fervor to intoxication.

This rumor reached the ears of St. Peter, who, filled with the Holy Ghost, rose up before the multitude and delivered a speech full of fervor and of logical truth. In a few, simple fearless words he addresses them: "Ye men of Judea and all that dwell in Jerusalem, be this known to you and with your ears receive my words." From this simple exordium, short yet fulfilling every precept for an exordium, he passes to a direct denial of the charge brought against the apostles.

He does not dwell long upon this refutation, for his own grand, imposing tones, the calmness of his voice, the logical force of his speech were all a direct answer to the charges brought against them.

Besides, it is but the third hour of the day, and the apostle reminds his audience that men are not usually filled with wine at that time.

Having thus completely answered the objections brought against them, and having given us what we may call the refutation of his speech, he enters without delay upon the subject he has most at heart. The desire that is gnawing at his heart, the wish that is burning in his breast, the hope that inflames his every action is—baptism for the Jews, baptism in Christ's name. But to win them to baptism he must prove that the Messiah has come, and that the Christ whom they have crucified is He.

This is really the proposition of his discourse, which can be reduced to this enthymeme, Jesus Christ is God, you, ought then, to believe in Him and be baptized in His name.

But here prudence plays her part; she forbids the direct announcement of his proposition—how could he preach Christ to this unbelieving people? It was no time for elaborate declamation. These souls were to be won to God—won to the infant church of Christ—but they must be convinced, first, that the Holy Ghost was to come ; secondly, that the time appointed for the fulfillment of the promised sanctifier had come, and, thirdly, that the results he would accomplish were precisely those they had witnessed in the apostles.

A passage from the prophet Joel is sufficient to establish these three truths, for the prophet had announced that the spirit of the Lord would be on all flesh, and that the servants of the Lord should tell the things that were to come. Who, moreover, could have failed to recall the scenes of the crucifixion, the darkness that was over the land, the strange sights that were seen in the land and the other marvels that had ushered in the morn of the Pentecost, as the dauntless apostle pictured the scenes described by the prophet Joel. These were to precede and accompany the Comforter when He came to abide on earth, and now that the Jews themselves had been witnesses of this, could they draw any other conclusion but that the time foreshadowed in prophecy had come to them?

And the result of the Comforter's coming was to be a strange enthusiasm, a kindling of the spirit, for "as an invisible wind, as an outpoured flood " would the Sanctifier come. It was this enthusiasm they had seen in the apostles, and which they in their unspiritual ways had charged to the fumes of wine.

By this wonderful passage St. Peter proves conclusively to the Jews that the apostles had received the Holy Ghost, and he closes this part of his speech with these words, so full of consolation and of life : "And it shall come to pass that whosoever shall call upon the name of the Lord shall be saved."

This brings the apostle step by step to the grand truth he is unveiling to the people. For he will now prove to them that the Lord, in whom salvation is promised, is the Messiah, and that the Messiah is none other than the Christ of Nazareth whom they have so ruthlessly killed.

This he establishes from three points: (a) From the testimony Christ has received from God; (b) by His indisputable resurrection, and (c) by His triumphant ascension.

Thus he brings forward the argument of his speech: He to whom God has borne testimony by a number of miracles, the Lord whom He has raised from the dead, whom He has elevated to heaven to a seat at His right hand, He is the promised and expected Redeemer ; but all these characteristics are found in Jesus of Nazareth; therefore, Jesus

of Nazareth is the promised Redeemer, and the chosen people of God
ought to seek baptism in His name.

Where can be found sounder logic? Where a grander example of
the development of an idea? Where a conclusion drawn more clearly
from established premises?

The apostle in speaking of the miracles of our Saviour, does not
speak of Him at first as the Son of God, but as man. "You know,"
he says, "that Jesus of Nazareth was a man, approved of God among
you by miracles and wonders and signs, which God did by Him in
the midst of you, as you also know." "Yet this is the man you have
put to death; this same being delivered up by the determinate counsel
and foreknowledge of God, you, by the hands of wicked men, have
crucified and slain."

St. Peter then proceeds to prove that this same Christ has risen from
the dead, and he does not hesitate to declare that if He has broken the
chains of death, it was because he was not subject to the empire of
death. "Whom God hath raised up, having loosed the sorrows of hell,
as it was impossible that he should be holden by it."

In support of this he cites the 50th psalm of the prophet: "I fore-
saw the Lord before my face: because he is at my right hand that I
may not be moved, for this my heart hath been glad, and my tongue
hath rejoiced; moreover, my flesh also shall rest in hope. Because thou
wilt not leave my soul in hell, nor suffer thy Holy One to see corruption. Thou hast made known to me the ways of life: Thou shalt
make me full of joy with thy countenance."

As, however, the Jews might object that this applied to David himself and not to Christ, St. Peter shows that this psalm did in reality
refer to Christ: "Ye men, brethren, let me fully speak to you of the
patriarch David; that he died and was buried and his sepulchre is
with us to the present day." David cannot, therefore, have spoken of

himself.   But more than this, his own life and words give us a clue to the person pointed out.   "Whereas, therefore, he was a prophet and knew that God had sworn to him with an oath, that of the fruit of his loins one should sit upon his throne.   Foreseeing this, he spoke of the resurrection of Christ.   For neither was he left in hell, neither did his flesh see corruption."

Now, declares St. Peter, with the firm tones of one who has both seen and heard what he is speaking of: "This Jesus hath God raised again, whereof all we are witnesses."   It is most natural after this for the orator to refer to Christ's wonderful ascension, and to proclaim that He has graciously lavished upon them the gifts of the Holy Ghost. "Being exalted, therefore, by the right hand of God, and having received of the Father the promise of the Holy Ghost, He hath poured forth that which you see and hear."

From this the apostle in the most skilful manner conceivable brings out the proposition of his speech.   For the ascension of Christ to the right hand of the Father and the descent of the Holy Ghost were so closely connected in the minds of the Jews, that the ascension of Christ proved He had sent the Comforter, and the coming of the Comforter proved that Christ had ascended into heaven.

It is only necessary, then, for him to firmly establish the ascension of Christ: "for David ascended not into heaven; but he himself said : 'The Lord said to my Lord, sit thou on my right hand, until I make thy enemies thy footstool.'"

In quoting this passage of the 109th psalm, the apostle emphatically points out that those who would attempt to apply these words to the prophet-king of old, would be under the necessity of asserting that David had ascended to heaven in bodily form.   This was so evidently untrue that no one would have ventured to make such a statement.   The prophet must, then, have spoke of the Messiah.   What other conclusion could be drawn by the Jews but that Jesus of Nazareth was the Messiah?

It is obvious from this that Christ was the Messiah, and this the apostle declares in a few energetic words: " Let all the house of Israel know most certainly, that God hath made both Lord and Christ, this same Jesus, whom you have crucified."

But if Jesus is the Messiah and the true Christ, if He is seated at the right hand of the Father He is God, for they have frequently heard him say: " I and the Father are one." So deeply has the fervid orator of the first Pentecost wrought upon his hearers, that they cried out to Peter and the rest of the apostles: "What shall we do, men and brethren?" What shall they do? Why, follow the logical outcome of his sermon, for he said to them : " Do penance and be baptized, every one of you, in the name of Jesus Christ, for the remission of your sins, and you shall receive the gift of the Holy Ghost."

Here, then, we have one of the most striking examples of the manner in which an orator may proceed to the gradual unfolding of a truth to which his hearers are openly opposed. To make the picture complete, we must bring before us the sturdy form of the sincere and warm-hearted apostle, aglow with the eloquence that is born of the spirit of God, the old impetuosity still there, but softened and chastened by the sad scenes of Calvary, while he speaks the message of glad tidings to the Jews and the nations of the earth.

The Speech may be outlined as follows :

Acts of the Apostles, 2d Chap., v. 14.

Exordium, Simple. { St. Peter wins the attention of his audience by asking for a patient hearing—(v. 14).

Confutation. { Refutes the slanderous charge brought against the apostles.—(v. 15:.

Proposition, not formally expressed. { Believe in Christ who is the Messiah.

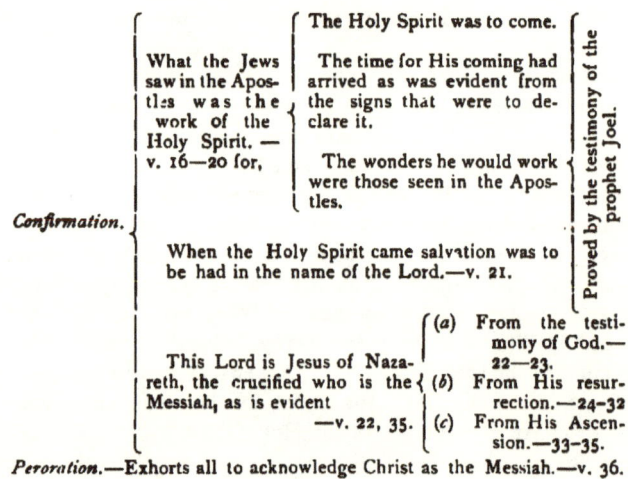

Confirmation.

What the Jews saw in the Apostles was the work of the Holy Spirit. — v. 16—20 for,

The Holy Spirit was to come.

The time for His coming had arrived as was evident from the signs that were to declare it.

The wonders he would work were those seen in the Apostles.

Proved by the testimony of the prophet Joel.

When the Holy Spirit came salvation was to be had in the name of the Lord.—v. 21.

This Lord is Jesus of Nazareth, the crucified who is the Messiah, as is evident —v. 22, 35.

(a) From the testimony of God.— 22—23.

(b) From His resurrection.—24-32

(c) From His Ascension.—33-35.

Peroration.—Exhorts all to acknowledge Christ as the Messiah.—v. 36.

Autobiography of a Snowflake

BEFORE I became a snowflake I was rolling and floating about in the vast ocean, where sometimes I was tossed around in the terrible storms, or at times an old whale or a steamer buffeted me in every way, but did not take any particular notice of me. I felt insulted at these many rebuffs, and I asked fiery Phoebus to free me from all my cares.

He received me with his usual congenial warmth, and as I looked at him I became dazzled by his brightness and the glittering of the diamonds and gems he wore, and gradually I felt myself raised up, becoming lighter, though I took up more space.

Higher and higher I rose in the world, and finally I reached a large cloud where I remained awhile traveling about with it. Sometimes it let fall a few drops of rain, and on the earth below might be seen the farmer hurrying to gather in his hay, or the urchin running home from school. One day it came to my turn, and I felt myself gradually becoming a liquid, and with other drops I began to descend through the air which was very cold. I became white in color, and looking around I saw that my companions were white also.

Now we descended slower and were blown about by the wind in all directions. I fell on a newly erected tombstone in a churchyard. There was no sound but the mournful sighing of the wind as it blew among some neighboring trees. I managed to see on the tombstone that it was erected to Mary ——, but when I came to the line where "aged" was written, and was about to read, the wind came along, as if to tell me to mind my business, and set me flying again in the air.

As I was whirled about, I could not help thinking of the inscription again, I wondered whether it was in memory of some grandmother of seventy, who had already received her share of life, or whether there were some children now crying for their mother or if there was a broken-hearted maiden mourning for her lover, or perhaps it was erected to some infant child whom God had called before she met with the dangers of life.

But soon my reverie was cut short, as I was blown against a large window of many colors. I saw that it was a window of a church and that the church was lit up, as I could tell by the light shining through the window. I could not account for the service at that hour, for it was but a little after midnight. Therefore, being very curious, I sidled down into one corner, and there through a crack I saw the altar, and the many men and women who occupied the pews. On the altar I saw the Catholic priest offering the sacrifice of the mass, and on one side of the altar there was a scene representing the stable at Bethlehem, and the birth of our Saviour. Then I understood that it was the midnight mass which Catholics celebrate every year, the night on which our Lord was born. I heard the "Gloria" sung as if by angels' voices, and when at the consecration all the heads were bowed in adoration, there came a heaven-like stillness and calmness over the place, and, as the tinkling of the elevation bell was heard, even the winds stood still, and the storm forgot to rage.

Thus I could go on and tell you what I saw and heard from that window corner, but again the burly Boreas interrupted me and tossed me about, only to stop on the window sill of a rich mansion. There I lay for awhile waiting for the curtain to be raised so that I could get a glimpse of the interior. Soon it was raised, and looking over the window sash I saw a merry group of children examining their numerous presents and all were happy and contented. In one part of the room a youthful jockey was riding his rocking horse, in another part a future general was practicing as a drummer boy.

While I was watching them at play, the house-maid opened the window and swept myself and my companions away. Descending I fell on the roof of a shanty, and looked through the crack. There also, was a group of children, and they were gladly inspecting their presents, though less numerous and less valuable. They were all joyous and happy indeed; everybody and everything seemed glad for it was Christmas-day, and it was on that day that the musical strains of angels' voices were heard years ago in Bethlehem, far away, singing "Glory to God in the highest and peace on earth to men of good will."

Soon I was blown from the roof, and a busy urchin picked me up with many other flakes and threw me at the driver of a sleigh which was going along by the river side. He missed the driver and when we became separated, I fell on the ice and glided to the other side of the stream where I lodged beneath the shelter of an overhanging rock. Here I remained for many days. Early in the morning I could see the snow birds flying around seeking food, later I listened to the children prattling as they wended their way to school, and when studies were over, I heard the ring of many pairs of skates on the clear ice and the merry shouts of the boys and girls, and one day—now don't tell—I heard Sarah Thompson and Sam Jones making love, as they were going to singing school, but that's a secret. When spring came, the ice melted away and feeling sorry I began to weep and I was rolled along with the rushing stream. Thus, as man from dust returns to dust, so I from water returned to water, and now I bid you farewell wishing you may have as merry a Christmas as I'did on the first day of my existence.

The Cricket's Soliloquy.

Well, the warm summer is over and I am settled in my winter home. How comfortable this warm, clean hearth is on this cold December night! Here I can sit and sing, as I watch the great logs blaze and smoulder and the new ones put on, which make this parlor as bright as the noonday sun.

I wonder what is the matter. There is so much hurrying to and fro, and many new arrivals and hearty welcomes, something unusual must be going on. I must keep my eyes and ears open, for I can see and hear everything from my little crevice in the chimney.

Why, I declare, they are moving the tables and chairs out of the way for a dance ; and here come the young people, their bright faces telling plainer than words of the grand fun they have been having. Dear old grandma has the armchair near the fire and very close to me. while father and mother are very busy and happy, arranging the gifts for the little ones. What a merry gathering! Brothers and sisters, aunts and uncles and cousins, are all determined to do their share to make this meeting a pleasant one.

There is the music now, and the young folks take their places, and they are turning round and round and marching backwards and forwards. Oh, my! I think I shall faint—they make me so giddy—the dance is more lively than ever; old and young enjoy it, but it makes my brain whirl. I think I'll take a peep at grandmamma.

She is receiving a great deal of attention, and takes off her glasses, rubs them as though desiring a better view, but I think it is to dry the tears of happiness that have dimmed them.

Dance after dance until the great hall clock begins to strike. What! Eleven o'clock! is it possible? Oh, dear me, it is very late for those sweet children to be up. But papa reminds them that they must now retire in order to rise in time for Mass.

"I must hang up my stocking," said one of the children. "So must I," "and I," and they tumbled out of the room, rolling over each other in their haste to get their stockings. They return, like well-drilled soldiers, advance in double quick time—but, O my! they are coming towards me. I think they see me; oh, dear, my heart is in my throat; they will kill me I know.—What a goose I am; they are only going to place a stocking up the chimney, and hastily scamper up stairs, saying as they go, "good night, good night" and "merry Christmas, merry Christmas."

Christmas, what is Christmas, I wonder? Hark, I hear footsteps; who is coming now? Father and mother, to be sure, loaded with packages of all sizes and shapes. "This for Charlie," says mamma, and a nice air gun finds its way clear to the toe of Charlie's stocking. "For Willie," says father, and he holds an elegant Rugby football at the top of Willie's stocking, but a glance tells him it would be vain to try to put that large football in Willie's sock, so he places it beside it. "For

Dannie," they read off, and something heavy and shining like silver is put with Dannie's stockings ; then a high, round box for Fannie, for grandma, for Uncle John, and so they go on, parcel after parcel, until their task is finished. With a glance to make sure everything was in its place, they leave the room and go up stairs.

The cricket thought that this was a fine opportunity to see all the nice things they had left in the room, so he took grandma's spectacles and went into fits of joy over the treasures until he came to Dannie's gift, shinning like a mirror. Oh ! a pair of skates," he cried. I wonder if I could skate ? I'll try. I will jump up to the top, it is so smooth. Help, brother crickets, I can't walk on it, and I can't see how to hold on. Oh ! help me—my eyes are dim—I have fallen and hurt my leg ; I hope I haven't broken the skate. I don't mind the leg, St. Jacob's oil will cure it—but to think of spoiling the nickle plating on those fine skates."

But this is Fannie's. How soft and warm this muff is ? When I have examined all the other things, I will creep back to this muff and take a good sleep before they come down. This is for grandma, a nice prayer book with large print, so plain that I could almost read it myself.

And here's a set of china for Katie with lovely flowers painted on them ; how I would so enjoy a cup of tea from one of these cups. Well, if Christmas brings all these beautiful things, I wish I had a Christmas too.

I wonder if crickets ever have a Christmas ; I think I'll have a party to-morrow and give away all the old things I have on hand. But I am very tired and sleepy and I can't look around any more. I'll have a pleasant night's sleep, however, in that soft muff. Oh ! it's just like velvet ; I hope I wake in time, as I don't want to be seen. Good night. Mr. Skate, good night, Mr. Rugby, I wish you a merry Christmas. and I'll let you come to the party if you only promise to be good.

The Island Bell.

IT WAS late in the autumn some years ago when we were grouped around the glowing fire with greater interest than usual to listen to one of my uncle's stories. "When we were running," he said, "from 'Frisco to Japan we met with a few storms which drove us considerably out of our course. The weather changed suddenly one day, and after about half a day's sail before a good stiff breeze, we sighted land. The chart did not indicate any land just here, so we headed in that direction in the hope of discovering a new country.

When we arrived there we found that it was only a small island, in fact a mere rock, whose only feature seemed to be an old, crumbling, grass-grown structure that looked to me as if it had been intended for a church steeple. The congregation probably being small, they had dispensed with the church itself. We wanted to make Yokohama as soon as possible, so we did not stop to make any explorations. However, when we were entering the harbor we happened to pick up a pilot who could speak English, so I told him of the island we had sighted. ' That,' said he, ' is an enchanted island. It was well you did not land or you might never have escaped. However, there is a term of three hours, just before midnight, on a certain day, when the spell is broken. If you had landed you would have perceived a door leading into the tower and entering you would see a monstrous statue, the lord of the island, dreaming. His ear is in the middle of his forehead ; he has neither eyes nor nose. At the top is a beautiful silver bell. The history of that island is this. It was formerly inhabited by people who came there I know not how, and who were unable to leave it ; yet, as long as they remained, they were doomed to mourn continually. Three times in the day a spirit would touch the bell with a golden hammer and each time every inhabitant of the enchanted island felt a blow on the head causing great pain.

Much as they would have liked to have avoided this, they bore it patiently, for if the bell remained silent for one day the people would be destroyed. For long years they lived there, till at noon of a certain day it was noticed that the bell did not ring. Immediately the people were apprehensive of danger. They all assembled and with loud prayers and many offerings asked the idol to tell them why the bell did not ring. After listening to them for a long time he moved slightly and said in a voice which shook the whole island : 'One of your number has entered my temple to seek to destroy my power. For this offense you must all perish.' Then all the people went out sadder than ever for in twenty-four hours they must die. At last one more enterprising than the others returned to the temple and asked the statue if nothing could be done to avert the calamity.

Then again the lord of the island spoke : 'There is, but if you mention what I say to anyone, it will come with tenfold bitterness to all the people. At three hours before midnight the spell of the island is broken. As soon as you are able to leave, take a skiff and direct your course northward. There is a ship sailing on the ocean. She will be struck with a storm. She will founder. Tied to a broken spar not far from the wreck you will find a sleeping child, who unlike you, has never known sorrow. Bring him to the door of my temple. Perform the incantation which you know and the spirit will appear and bring the child to me.' Impatiently does the hero wait his time, for he knows that once free from this island he is safe from the power of the idol. Accordingly, when the time has arrived he puts out in a small skiff and directs his course northward to where he knows the ship will pass. But he has not gone far when he perceives the mast of a ship floating in the water. Coming up to it he finds a child lashed to it. Then the remembrance of his sorrowful brothers comes before his mind, and he remembers that by bringing this child to the temple their lives would be saved. Immediately he takes him into the boat and rows for the island. He is tired and his progress is slow. The storm moves southward and overtakes him.

Shortly after midnight he arrived at the island but it is impossible to land in such a storm. He stands in the boat and while he urges it ashore with one hand. in the other he grasps the child ready to jump into the angry waves, if the boat strikes a rock. The storm grows wilder. His boat is dashed against the rock and destroyed. He is tossed about pitilessly by the wild waves. In endeavoring to protect the child from harm he meets the same fate as the skiff. The child alone floats upon the wild waves. He awakes to feel the cold water around him and hear the thunder roar. He screams, then sinks under the waves, and thus ends that life but lately begun. At sunrise the bodies of the child and the man appear on the beach surrounded by the fragments of wreck of the foundered ship. But the people are too busily engaged, to give the dead burial. They are thinking of their doom soon to be sealed.

The bell continued to remain silent till the sun had reached the meridian, and the air began to darken, it gave forth faint murmurs for the whole island was being shaken by a great earthquake. The people crowded into the temple where the statue menacingly addressed them in a thundering voice. Then the floor of the temple and opened with a loud shriek they sink from sight. "And now, children, it is time for bed," he said, rising. "But, uncle," one asked, "if they all died how did the pilot find this out?" "Well, now, do you think I would insult the Japanese who told me by asking him such a question?" answered uncle, as he rose and left the room.

Monumentum ære Perennius.

RICHARD S. FARLEY,
LOUIS D. CONLEY,
DANIEL I. BRADLEY,
FORBES J. HENNESSY,
PHILIP R. HILDRETH,
WILLIAM H. GOOD,
ROBERT P. GREEN,
JAMES P. GLYNN,
EDWARD J. BEARY,
HENRY E. O'KEEFE,
EDWARD F. DENNER,
JOHN D. KING,
JOHN P. LYNCH,
HENRY W. MCLAUGHLIN,
WILLIAM J. DAINTY,
JOSEPH A. MCALEENAN,
JOHN S. MCALEENAN,
CHARLES J. PARKS,
ROBERT G. EMMET,
STUART N. CLARKE.
BERNARD J. CONVILLE.
JOHN H. DOODY,
DAVID A. MURRAY,
JOSEPH P. MCCORMICK,
ARTHUR J. KENNY,
JOSEPH I. FOLEY,
JAMES SIMCOX,
TIMOTHY V. MENTON,
JOHN E. MCHUGH,
JOSEPH A. HAGGARTY,
W. ARTHUR BOONE,
AUG. THIERY,
JOSEPH A. MULRY,
JOHN J. MOONEY,
LOURDES H. DOWLING,
PETER W. MAGUIRE,
PATRICK CASTLES,

FRANCIS X. HENNESSY,
JOSEPH D. CREEDEN,
WILLIAM J. MCCONVILLE,
EDWARD J. DELANEY,
SHERIDAN S. NORTON,
JAMES I. MOAKLEY,
TIMOTHY J. MURRAY,
FRANCIS T. HUGHES,
HAROLD H. O'CONNOR,
EDWARD J. TIERNEY,
FERDINAND J. BRAHM,
THOMAS P. WALSH,
MYLES J. TIERNEY,
JOHN S. GAFFNEY,
BENJAMIN KEILY,
JOSEPH CUSHING,
DAVID KENNEDY,
PETER A. LEE,
HUGH O'REILLY,
PETER B. HAVANAGH,
WM. P. O'FLAHERTY,
JOSEPH F. SMITH,
WILLIAM J. SMYTH,
JOHN J. BRODERICK,
JOHN M. DAILY,
MICHAEL F. HENNESSY,
JOHN F. DOWLING,
MARTIN BUCKLEY,
DANIEL J. EARLEY,
VINCENT R. ZOLNOWSKI,
G. CLINTON MILLER,
HENRY F. DEMENA,
JOHN J. TRAINOR,
AUSTIN J. HEALY,
FAUSTINO LOZANO,
JOSEPH MCMAHON,
CHARLES ORMSBY,

J. FITZGERALD.

www.ingramcontent.com/pod-product-compliance
Lightning Source LLC
Chambersburg PA
CBHW020758020726
47495CB00008B/2492